HIS STRENGTH TO STAND

THE BRIDES OF PURPLE HEART RANCH BOOK 11

SHANAE JOHNSON

Copyright © 2021, Ines Johnson. All rights reserved.
This novel is a work of fiction. All characters, places, and incidents described in this publication are used fictitiously, or are entirely fictional. No part of this publication may be reproduced or transmitted, in any form or by any means, except by an authorized retailer, or with written permission of the author.

Edited by Alyssa Breck

First Edition July 2021

cool breeze blew into the window. The tendrils of fresh valley air brushed through the room, ruffling the pages of a calendar that hung on the wall. When the pages settled down, the fourth day on the calendar was circled with a big, red O.

May the Fourth. The fourth—or rather, the force—certainly was with Paul Hanson today, his favorite day of the year. Paul loved everything Star Wars, including the franchise's true hero—his namesake Han Solo.

It wasn't Luke who got the girl in the end. It was Han who scored the beautiful and highly capable Leia. Luke had been born a hero. Meanwhile, Han's character arced from outlaw to rebel alliance. So really, who took an actual hero's journey?

Outside the window, Paul saw his best friend Luke Jackson—and no, the irony wasn't lost on either of them that they had become best friends in spite of their names. Luke had his wife wrapped up in a tight embrace and was going in for the kiss.

Paul played voyeur for perhaps a second longer than was proper. Finding a love of his own was next on his agenda, now that he had his health in order. He'd had faith that his body would heal, and it had. The same faith told him that love was just around the corner for him.

Turning back to the calendar, Paul noted that the circle he'd drawn wasn't a perfect O. The ending point didn't touch the starting point. It more so overlapped it. Also, the bottom half of the O was heavier than the top, as though the ink had gotten tired halfway into its journey.

Still, the shape did its duty. It marked the important date. His final day here at the Purple Heart Ranch.

The rehabilitation ranch for wounded soldiers had been a haven for Paul. He'd come to the ranch with reluctance. But one look at the wide-open spaces, and Paul had felt like he'd come home.

True, Montana was as far away from home as he could get. He was a Florida boy, born and bred. Being landlocked in the middle of the country without the ocean in sight should've made him feel claustrophobic. Instead, it had the opposite effect on him. He'd felt free.

The horseback riding had been his favorite. When he sat atop a horse, not a single pain from his battle injuries bothered him. He and the horse became one, and Paul could fly again.

He'd fallen so in love with the horses that he'd signed on to be a ranch hand at the Vance Ranch next door. Which meant this move would be over and done with in an hour, and he could get on with the rest of his life tending to the small stable of horses at the cattle ranch.

It was the perfect job for him. He could be out of doors. He could work with horses. And he could be independent. Bonus, there was even a creek that bordered the property. So, if he pretended really hard, he could almost, kinda, sorta imagine he was back home on the Florida coast.

The horses next door needed him. Most of the people on that ranch were focused on the cattle, which was how the ranch made its money. But Paul would be there solely for the horses. It was going to feel good to be needed. To be a leader again.

Paul bent down to pick up a moving box. He hadn't come here with much, so it was only filled with a few game boards. Board games were his second favorite pastime.

"Hey! Drop it."

With a sigh, Paul straightened and held up his hands. He turned with his hands up and his mouth turned down. Luke stood in the doorway like a hovering mother.

"It's only three months after your surgery," Luke henpecked. "You're not supposed to lift heavy objects."

"I've been cleared for weeks," Paul said, trying to rein in his patience. He knew his best friend meant well, but the man could nag worse than his mother. "It's a ten-pound box."

"This is at least twenty-five pounds," Luke said, easily hefting the box filled with cardboard and plastic game pieces. "The other guys are coming to get the rest."

Paul opened his mouth to argue, but the room filled with other soldiers from the ranch. It was too many against one, so he clammed up. At least on

Vance Ranch, he wouldn't be treated with kid gloves. They only knew the basics of his injury and had only known him since his recovery.

"You sure you don't want to stay?" asked Dylan Banks, the founder of the Purple Heart ranch and one of its permanent residents.

"I can't pay the price tag," said Paul.

The other guys laughed. Any veteran's stay at the rehabilitation ranch was free. At least for the first three months. After that, the price tag to stay at the ranch wasn't monetary. It was matrimonial.

Paul liked the ladies. And they liked him back. But he had yet to meet his Leia.

Dating hadn't been at the top of his daily to-do lists. Not with the chronic pain from his injuries. Paul had had every intention of powering through the daily pain until the day he literally could take it no more. That day three months ago, the pain had hit him so hard that he'd passed out cold.

When he'd woken up, the doctors and his best friend insisted the damage wasn't something a horse ride or prayer could fix. Surgery was his only option.

Three months post-op and the pain had lessened. But in truth, it was still there most days. It was manageable if he popped a couple of aspirin in the morning. And sometimes again in the late afternoon. At night, he often cheated on NyQuil with a steaming mug of chamomile tea, but Paul suspected they knew about each other and talked while he slept peacefully. Well, mostly peacefully. Except when he woke up in the middle of the night with twinges of pain.

"You could always come and stay with me and Elaine," said Luke.

"Nah, I'm good."

Paul had said those words after Luke had rescued him from an explosion. He'd said them a few times after that life-altering incident. Each time he'd uttered the words, they'd been a lie.

Luke had already packed and moved out a week ago, when he'd married Elaine Reynolds, the town librarian, after only two months of dating. The couple had offered Paul a place in their brownstone in town. Paul had declined. It was a step shy of moving back in with his parents.

"I don't know if you realized this or not, but I am a grown man," Paul said. "I don't need you to babysit me, buddy."

Luke had probably saved Paul's life back in the military. Right before the explosion detonated, Luke had thrown his body over Paul's. The problem was, there had been a metal pipe on the ground that had made contact with Paul's low back. That's when the pain had started. It's also when Luke morphed into a helicopter mom, hovering over Paul like he was taking the SATs.

His friends had his cabin on the ranch cleared out in twenty minutes. That's how long it took to pack up his life. Paul took a step to the door. His hands were empty, but there was a sensation growing in his low back.

The twinge was a familiar sensation. He knew that the pain would pass if he gave it a moment. It always did.

Except this time, it didn't.

With all the contents of his medicine cabinet packed into one of the boxes, Paul realized he wouldn't be able to get to a couple of aspirin in time to tame the pain. As though it knew it wouldn't meet any resistance, the ache grew into agony. The agony burst into a burn.

And then it all went away.

Surprised at the quick surrender, Paul tried to take a second step forward. But it felt as though his legs had gone out under him.

They hadn't. But all the feeling had.

The next thing Paul knew, he was crashing to the ground. He heard shouts coming toward him. Luke's voice boomed over him the same way it had when the bomb went off back in the war zone. And then everything went black.

CHAPTER TWO

adison Gray's Manolo Blahnicks smacked down against the pavement. The pavement smacked back. A cloud of dirt à la Pig Pen from the Charlie Brown comic strip swirled up, fairly licking at her expensive shoes. Madison hopped away from the cloud, but she wasn't quick enough. The dark dirt settled on her pastel pumps.

"You gotta pay your fare, ma'am," called the taxi driver from the front of the orange sedan.

Madison balked at the three-digit number on the meter. It cost half that to go from JFK to anywhere in New York City. But she wasn't in the Big Apple any longer. She had flown from JFK out into the middle of nowhere. She'd known that leaving would come at a cost, and she would have to pay it.

The driver frowned at the piece of plastic she handed him. "Cash only."

Cash? As in dollar bills? Who carried actual currency around these days?

Actually, she did. She'd grabbed a few hundred from the ATM before she'd boarded the plane. She'd pocketed the money for such emergencies as tipping porters at the airport, tipping handlers at the hotel she would be staying at, and tipping drivers to give her lifts until she got a car of her own. Madison handed over the entire wad of cash. She was sure there was an ATM inside the hospital.

The taxi pulled off in another plume of Pig Pen dirt tornado. Madison hopped out of the way, tugging her purse behind her back so that it wouldn't collect any dust in its now empty confines. When the soil and sediment settled, she turned and looked at her new place of business; Mercy General Hospital out in the middle of nowhere, Montana.

It was a long way away from the emergency rooms of New York City, where she'd cut her teeth on elite clientele, state-of-the-art technology, and cases worthy of medical journals. Mercy was also a VA Hospital, so there wasn't the latest tech available.

Which was a shame. The government should be funneling in as many tax dollars as possible to care for the men and women who served this country.

Well, today, at least, they were getting the best orthopedic surgeon on staff.

Madison walked up to the reception area. She offered the haggard-looking nurse her most winning smile. Which the woman didn't see as she cradled two phones in one hand and scribbled on a pad with the other.

Madison waited patiently while she looked around. There was a woman who sat in a wheelchair. Both her legs were lost, but there was no frown on her face. She looked out the window at the flower patch bordering the walkway.

Across from her sat a man. He had all his limbs. But his features contorted in a grimace of chronic pain. Beside him sat a child who clutched at a stuffed animal.

Madison's gaze held on the child. Pain she knew how to mitigate. Loneliness and abandonment whether a parent was there or far away, she had no cure for. Solitude had been a constant friend of hers growing up with a four-star general for a father. Tutors and private schools and, finally, boarding schools did not fill that void.

"Yes, can I help you?"

Madison turned back to the nurse. She inhaled, pulling her winning smile back on, the smile that she was Doctor Madison Gray, and nothing fazed her. "I'm Dr. Madison Gray and—"

"Right." The nurse turned from her, shifting the phones into the opposite hand. She grabbed a manilla envelope and shoved it toward Madison. "The chief said you'd be coming today. He's in a meeting with another candidate for Chief of Orthopedics."

Another candidate for Chief of Orthopedics? There was no other candidate for Chief of Orthopedics. She was *the* candidate for Chief of Orthopedics.

"There must be a mistake," Madison started. "You see, I'm Madison Gray-"

"If you'll just take a seat, Dr. Gray, I'll call you when he's ready for you."

The nurse placed one of the phones to her ear and began another conversation, summarily dismissing Madison. Though Madison stood bewildered long enough for the nurse to place the other phone to her ear and embark on yet another conversation.

Finally, Madison was able to regain her wits. She turned to the chairs in the waiting room. The father and son had vacated the chairs. Madison walked over and took the kid's empty seat.

What was going on?

She felt like she did when she'd earned the Valedictorian spot at her boarding school, and her father had failed to show to hear her speech. Or the time when she'd earned the Valedictorian spot after her bachelor's and her father had failed to show to see her walk across the stage. No, no, this was definitely more like that time she'd earned the Valedictorian spot in medical school, and her father had shown, but he'd spent the time on his cell phone talking to the Pentagon.

Steve Pena was the Chief of Medicine at Mercy. He'd been her teacher in med school. She'd been his star student. Only ever falling second a couple of times to He Who Shall Not Be Named. Pena had fairly groomed her for this job. And yet, she wasn't his first pick. She wasn't even his only pick.

Who could it possibly be? Likely some home-town boy who'd moved up the ranks of Mercy General.

The sound of two men laughing filled Madison's ears. Both laughs were familiar to her. One was the chief. The other she wouldn't name.

The man whose name she wanted to forget came

around the corner first. Doug Lamb's golden locks shone brighter than the sun. But his blond was harsh and hard for her to look at. He still had those sharp blue eyes that pierced into any woman's soul.

That was the problem. Doug's clear blue gaze wasn't discriminating. It would latch onto any woman in the vicinity, regardless of whether it was his girlfriend or not.

Those blue eyes latched onto Madison now. That grin grew impossibly bigger, brighter. *All the more to eat you with, my pretty.* But Madison was no longer naïve enough to follow a wolf into the woods.

"Madison, you made it," said Pena.

Madison rose to greet him, allowing him to kiss both her cheeks. The country seemed to be doing the old man well. He'd lost the pudgy belly he'd had back during his tenure in medical school. He looked lean and happy and at least ten years younger.

"Give me one second to check my messages, and then we'll chat," he said, turning to talk to the nurse behind the reception desk.

When Doug came in for a kiss, Madison took a step back. She'd sworn he would never kiss her again, and Madison was a woman of her word. Unlike him.

Doug's grin didn't falter. "You look surprised I'm here, Madison."

"I was looking forward to never seeing you again, actually," she said brightly, with a harsh glare in her eyes.

"Sorry to disappoint," said Doug. He wasn't.

"Aren't you supposed to be in California moving your way up the ranks of some Beverly Hills boutique hospital?"

"California has a lot of great doctors. But I couldn't pass up the opportunity to work with Doctor Pena again. Besides, you don't mind a little friendly competition?"

Friendly? She was going to tell him what he could do with his friendliness when the doors to the front entrance swung open with a gust of hot air. The sound of boots on the ground reminded Madison of standing beside her dad during a military demonstration. Looking up, she was sure those men marching into the door were all soldiers. So was the man they carried in as though he was a warrior fallen in some great battle.

"We need help," one of the soldiers barked out the order.

Madison didn't think. She jolted into action, grabbing a wheelchair. She pushed it over to the man. But once she got close, Doug tugged it from her grasp.

Was he serious right now? He was already trying to poach her job. Now he was going to poach this patient. Not today, Satan.

Madison didn't loosen her grip on the wheelchair. Doug didn't let go. A small tug of war ensued as the patient's eyes opened.

"I'll let you two fight it out," said the man. "I can just crawl to the intake desk."

*I*t was a lie. Paul couldn't crawl. He'd need the use of his knees to crawl. There was no feeling in his left leg at all. The right one felt like a million little pins and needles were stabbing into it all at the same time.

Man, was this the perfect time to look like an invalid or what? He'd dreamed this moment. Where most people had the dream of walking into class naked and there being a test, Paul had nightmares of being helpless in front of a beautiful woman.

And, man, was this woman beautiful. Skin the color of caramel macchiato, as though there were both rich dark chocolate and heavy cream in her lineage. Hazel eyes that were bright and intelligent. A set of full lips that looked ripe for kissing.

He'd never wanted to kiss someone so much in his life. Except he couldn't stand to get close to her mouth. He was useless in his friends' hold, as Luke commandeered the wheelchair from the warring medical professionals.

As always, Luke swept in to save the day. Meanwhile, Paul was Han Solo frozen in carbonate while Leia duked it out with Jaba the Hut.

"It's fine, nurse," Paul began as he used his upper arm strength to shove himself into the wheelchair. "Not all of me is down."

He grinned up at her. But then those hazel eyes shot a dagger at him.

"It's *Doctor* Gray," she enunciated each word.

And, now, not only was Paul naked, unprepared for the quiz, and incapacitated, he had just proven himself a chauvinist pig. What he wouldn't give to be an unintelligible Wookie right now. The groan that escaped him might've gotten him the role.

"What are the symptoms?" asked the guy she'd battled with. There was a raspy quality to his voice, which reminded Paul of Darth Vader.

The Vader guy looked every bit a doctor. From his black, polished wingtip shoes that had likely never seen a day on a battlefield to his pristine collared shirt, which blood wouldn't dare sully.

Paul decided he hated the man. That seemed like the right call when Dr. Gray's hazel eyes turned their daggers on Dr. Darth, giving Paul a relief. *Good, the enemy of my enemy might make the cute doctor my friend.* Paul turned back to Dr. Gray. But before he could open his mouth, his mom spoke up.

"He was in three months ago for a microdiscectomy," said Luke. "He's been doing PT and making progress. But I suspect he's been overdoing it. We were packing today, and he just collapsed."

"I didn't collapse, Mom," said Paul, huffing like a middle schooler whose mother insisted on walking him to his first day of class. "My leg just went numb."

"Which leg?" asked Dr. Gray.

"The left one."

Long, slender fingers reached down to prod his leg. Paul wanted to curse anything holy that he couldn't feel this angel's touch. Then she reached for his right leg.

"Does this one tingle?"

Paul sighed, unable to answer in the affirmative. Not because his leg had stopped tingling. The pins and needles he'd felt for the last hour turned to a herd of bees stinging him. Except in his mind's eye, he saw butterfly wings surrounding each stinger.

Dr. Gray's gaze connected with his. Her eyes were perfectly symmetrical. The corners of her long lashes swooped into a curve, just like a butterfly would.

"Any pain when you try to lift something?" Dr. Vader's raspy voice made them both wince.

"I didn't lift anything," Paul answered, wishing he had a light saber to be done with the fallen Jedi. But he was the outlaw with a pistol. So, of course, the man who thought he was a living, breathing Jedi knight had to step in.

"He lifted a twenty-five-pound box right before this happened," Luke said to Vader.

"It was maybe five pounds at the most," Paul said to Dr. Gray.

But she wasn't looking at him. She glared at Vader. Which was totally a Leia thing to do. Except the glare wasn't paternal. It looked like there was a different kind of relationship going on there.

"I'm his doctor," Dr. Gray hissed to Vader.

"You don't have privileges here yet, Madison. You haven't signed the paperwork."

"So, now you're not only a cheat with other women, you're going to start poaching my patients as well?"

Yup, definitely not a paternal thing happening. Looked like Vader had been seduced by the dark side. Paul couldn't imagine anything calling him away from a force as bright as Madison Gray.

"I do have other symptoms, Dr. Gray," Paul cut in, wanting her attention focused solely on him. It was only fair since he was caught in her gravitational pull.

She turned back to him with a grateful tilt to her perfectly arched brows. "What are they, Mr. ...?"

"Paul, you can call me Paul." He grinned at her then. It was the grin that stopped women walking on the street. It was the grin that got him out of a speeding ticket, a parking ticket, and detention in high school.

But Madison Gray wasn't looking at his mouth. She wasn't even looking at his face. She was peering down at his legs.

"Symptoms?" she prompted.

"Racing heart," said Paul.

She reached into what looked like a pricey designer handbag. Paul only knew because he'd seen many a senator or diplomat's wife or daughter with the large, busy patterned bag. They had cosmetics in there. Dr. Gray pulled out a pink stethoscope.

She breathed on the metal part, warming it up before placing the device on his heart. The spiraling curls of her hair tickled his nose as she leaned close. Paul inhaled. She smelled of the sweetest ripe apples.

"There are also little birds chirping," he said. "And hearts floating around."

Dr. Gray straightened. She peered at him. "Maybe we'll need a psych consult as well."

"Why?" grinned Paul. "You think a man falling in love is crazy?"

She blinked once, twice. But Paul caught it. There was the tiniest tug at the corner of her mouth. He hoped that was amusement and not a clinical assessment.

They stared each other off. She was Leia rebuffing Han's advances. She looked every bit the pampered princess. Paul felt like an unworthy space rat.

"What I think," she said, "is that you have a pinched nerve causing spinal degeneration. I think you're going to need another surgery, either artificial disc replacement or spinal fusion."

Paul turned her words over in his head. He met Luke's gaze first. The man ran his hands through his hair to expose his worry lines. Paul's gaze swept past to Dr. Vader. The man's hands were clenched into fists as though he wanted to put someone in a telekinetic choke hold

Finally, Paul turned back to Dr. Gray. "I want a second opinion."

CHAPTER FOUR

Madison knew she was attractive. But only because her mother had been beautiful. Lois Gray had been second runner-up in a Miss America pageant before she'd gotten married. When looking at old photographs of her mother, Madison saw shades of her own profile. Artfully applied makeup and tailored clothing helped color in the lines to round out her appearance.

So Madison was used to being hit on. By construction workers as she walked down the streets of New York City. By businessmen as she lunched at exclusive restaurants and artists as she tried out little-known hole in the wall dives. In the halls of the hospitals, attendings often tried to play doctor with her. She'd even had a few of the male nurses and technicians shoot their shot. Too bad for them that her dad was a general, and she expertly shot each one down.

The soldier's come on had been cute. Unexpected. And just a little charming.

Madison couldn't decide if it was bravado that ushered the words out of his mouth? The man had come into the doors helpless, having to be carried by his friends. But the grin on his face seemed undaunted.

It had to be an act to cover his fears of his condition.

Or a delusion.

Whichever it was, it was out of her department. Though she hadn't called psych. Yet. Madison was far more interested in getting a crack at Major Paul Hanson's back first.

"He's showing clear signs of degenerative disc disease," she said, pointing to Major Hanson's medical chart. "See here, the bone where the initial injury occurred is unstable."

"But he's already had a discectomy," Doug interjected. "His body is still adjusting. Give it time to restabilize, and the injured segment will likely resolve on its own with no need for further surgery."

"Or it could get worse and lead to permanent damage," Madison said through gritted teeth.

"Or you just want to cut into a patient unnecessarily."

"I'm a surgeon."

"Exactly. You see a problem, and you want to cut it."

Was that hurt in his voice? Not possible. Madison rounded on him. And yes, there it was. Doug wore his pouty face, the one where she wanted to grab a slice of pizza from the street vendor around the corner, but he wanted sushi from the newest high-end restaurant. Back when they were dating, she'd always cave, get dressed up, wait for a taxi to take them across town, and then eat unsatisfying blobs of rice and barely cooked fish.

Well, not today. She was having greasy pizza, and she didn't care how low his lip drooped.

"Are you two going to be able to work together?" Chief Pena rubbed at the salt and pepper stubble on his chin as he regarded the two of them. "You've never let your personal life interfere in your professional life before."

That's because Madison had always thought they were on the same side, even when they were each other's competition. They'd alternated first and second place in school and then jockeyed for position at the hospital where they were interns. But like a dummy, she'd mistaken their fierce competitiveness for love. She didn't realize until it was too late that Doug was more interested in being at the top of everyone's mind, not necessarily the best at what he did. And that included having the attention of other women because he certainly hadn't been the best boyfriend.

But that was over. So very, very over. This wasn't a popularity contest. This job was all about skill. And they all knew that Doug was the best at getting noticed, but she was the best at getting it done. He didn't stand a chance at the Chief of Orthopedic Surgery position.

"Just a passionate discussion over a case," Madison said with her winning smile. "You've seen worse between us in your classroom."

A smile full of nostalgia crossed Chief Pena's face as he nodded. Then he picked up the paperwork and frowned. "Major Hanson was under our care just a few months ago. He was seen by the last Chief of Ortho. It looks like we missed something. If I remember correctly, Major Hanson was against surgery then. I doubt he's changed his mind now."

"Well, that's my job as his doctor," said Madison.

"To present him with all the data and advice so that he can make the best choice and course of action."

"Not so fast, Madison," said Doug. "The patient asked me for my opinion. And I say we need more details. Let's start with an MRI."

"Doug's right," said Pena.

Madison dug her nails into her palm to keep from shouting.

"We do need more information to help the patient make the best decision," the chief continued. "Not all soldiers want surgery. And in this case, if we've made a surgical error, it's going to be bad for us. We need to handle this case with the utmost care."

Madison understood that sentiment. When her father had been injured in the line of duty, he'd resisted any medical intervention, insisting that he could walk it off. He'd been wrong. That bravado had cost him his life, where a simple surgery might have prolonged it.

"We need to go in and do our due diligence on this one. Look at every x-ray twice. Triple check each chart."

"Yes, chief," said Doug, but his gaze was on her.

"Understood," said Madison, holding Doug's blue stare.

The smile on both their faces was the same one when they wished one another luck on an exam, knowing full well they hoped the other got an answer wrong. But Madison was going to ace this exam. She was going to get the top grade.

"And chief," Madison went on, "what about filling the Chief of Orthopedic Surgery position?"

Chief Pena's fingers went back to stroking the gray hairs on his chin. He looked between the two of them again. "I had originally been ready to offer you the job, Madison. But when Doug showed interest, I couldn't pass up the opportunity to have two of my best students on staff."

Doug nodded his head as though he actually agreed with Pena. But Madison saw right through it. He wasn't here for the job. He was here to take it from her.

Be it a misguided attempt to win her back? Or a final sucker punch after his infidelity? She wasn't sure which, and she didn't care. Because she actually wanted this job.

A chance to work with veterans. To do the work for the men and women of this country who really needed her expertise. To perform the surgeries that would've saved her father's life, that's why she was here. Not for some silly rivalry with her ex-boyfriend.

Doug turned to her with a smile that used to make her heart fluttery like butterfly wings. But instead of seeing birdies and hearts floating around her head, she saw arrows aimed at a goal.

"May the best man win," said Doug.

Her GPA was one-tenth of a point higher than his. The recommendations he'd gotten had said that he was *great*. Her recommendations from the same faculty had said *stellar*.

So Madison didn't doubt the best man would win. And it would be her. She just needed to convince a scalpel-shy soldier to let her cut him open. Easy.

CHAPTER FIVE

The sound of boots impacting the ground brought Paul awake. He knew he wasn't overseas on the battlefield. There was no smell of burnt carbon from gunfire, or sulfur from explosives, or iron from fresh blood. The place he was in smelled of antiseptic cleaners. Because he was in a hospital room. The last place in the world he wanted to be.

His immediate response was to hit the ground and run. But he couldn't. He couldn't even lift his legs to move from the bed. The pins and needles pain was gone. Laying in the bed, Paul felt nothing below his waist.

He didn't open his eyes. He wasn't ready to face

the possibility that he might never walk again. The very notion felt like a lie to him.

Something in his heart told him he would walk. That he would walk right past this trial. It was his faith.

Paul had felt that same calling to serve in the military. Yes, he went to fight for his country. But he also went to lend his strength to those souls who couldn't defend themselves. Paul had felt a niggling that his work was nearing completion just before the bomb that ended his time in service went off.

He'd known in that deep well inside of himself that that door was closed for him. He also felt a nagging that another was opening. He felt certain of his new path the first time he climbed on a horse. He knew with the same certainty that he would ride again. He just had to get out of this hospital first.

The thumping of soles on the ground continued. *Thump, thump, thump, squeak.* And then again, and again. The incessant noise finally forced Paul's eyes open to Luke, pacing the length of the small hospital room. The man reached one wall, then turned on his heel to march back to the other side.

"Will you sit down? You're making me dizzy," said Paul.

That wasn't the truth. Paul was lying prone, and

he didn't feel anything. He should be the one panicking. But Luke was doing it well enough for the both of them.

"The doctors haven't been by here yet," said Luke. "The nurse said they'd be by this morning. It's almost afternoon."

The nurse had informed them that the doctors were reviewing his charts. Dr. Madison Gray and… Paul hadn't bothered remembering who the second one was. He regretted that he'd asked for that second opinion. Especially if it meant that he wouldn't get to see Madison Gray again.

She was the bright spot in all of this. He needed a little brightness now. The sky outside offered him none. There were too many clouds in the way of the star out there.

"Maybe I should go and find the nurse?" said Luke. "To see what the holdup is?"

The man had stopped his pacing and was now sitting in the lone chair in the room. Luke's long body folded awkwardly on the four-legged apparatus. He tried straightening his legs, but they hit the edge of Paul's bed. He folded them, but his knees bumped a tray.

There was a part of Paul that wanted to revel in his best friend's discomfort. Maybe that would get him to leave the room. But Paul knew better. Luke would stay with him, no matter what. This behavior went beyond what a best friend would do. Luke did it because he and Paul were family.

Paul knew Luke still felt responsible for his injury. But at the end of the day, Luke had saved his life. Nearly at the expense of his own. Just a few more meters and Luke would've been in the blast zone, blown to bits and no longer hovering over Paul.

"It'll likely be another surgery," said Luke.

Paul barely kept in his groan. Truth be told, he'd rather face another bomb or pipe to the back than a surgery. He'd gone under the knife once. He did not want to go back down that road.

His body apparently agreed with him. At the mention of the word *surgery*, the tingles returned to both his legs. The return of the feeling in his lower extremities gave credence to Paul's belief that this paralysis was just a temporary setback. Likely his body working out the kinks of the injury. It would pass, just as all pain did. There was no need to cut him open. He just needed time.

What he did know was that whatever was going wrong with his body now, it would derail all of his plans if it didn't resolve soon. He wouldn't be able to work at the Vance Ranch now, not when he couldn't be relied on to stand.

Neither could he go back to the Purple Heart Ranch. His time there had run out. Unless he got married.

But that was a no-go. Not because Paul had no desire to marry. Despite all his flirting, he wanted a wife and family of his own. But not until he knew for certain he could perform as a husband and father should.

He should be able to sweep a woman off her feet if he wanted to make her a wife. He should be able to carry her over the threshold of their home. He should be able to chase after any tykes he brought into this world.

A knock sounded at the door. Paul's heart jumped. But when the door opened, he didn't see a dark-haired bun with spirals trying to escape the hold. He saw slicked-back blond hair.

"Mr. Hanson," said Dr. Vader.

"It's Major," Paul corrected. The doctor worked in a hospital that catered to vets. and he didn't bother to use their rank? That was strike one against him.

"Right, Major." Then the man mock saluted with

a grin. "I've been looking at your chart, and it tells me it's possible you don't need surgery."

Paul perked up at that. He could get out of here, likely sooner rather than later.

"This is all possibly your body still working out issues from your initial injury and the first surgery."

Huh? Paul's estimation of this doctor was growing. But he knew better than to be easily led by the dark side of the force.

"Still, I want to run some more tests to be sure."

Tests would mean sticking around. Sticking around would mean he'd likely bump into the pretty surgeon again. Dr. Vader droned on, using big words that Paul didn't understand while wearing a smirk that said he knew he was the smartest person in the room.

Paul wasn't interested in that particular measuring contest. He leaned to the side to peer over Vader's shoulder. But he didn't catch sight of Madison Gray.

"… I think that would be the best course of action."

Paul blinked his attention back to the male doctor before him. He hadn't heard a word the man said. Didn't matter. "Thanks for your opinion, doc. I'll talk it over with my actual doctor."

"I am your doctor."

Paul only just held in his snort. The way the man said that sounded way too much like Vader telling Luke that he was his father.

"No, you gave me a second opinion. Dr. Gray is my doctor. I'd like her opinion on your opinion. Where is she?"

CHAPTER SIX

Yesterday had been a long day of travel. The four-star hotel had had a two-star mattress. And she was still waiting on the bulk of her wardrobe to arrive. And, now, the day was stretching into forever as Madison tried to dig herself out of all the case files she'd just been assigned.

There was a backlog. Patient wait times for simple procedures were simply unacceptable. But that was nothing compared to a mile-long list of patients who needed more sophisticated procedures, which simply weren't possible at this facility that was over fifty years old.

Still, Madison dug into the problem like the documents were a sickness that she was going to root out. By the time lunch hit, she had only come away with a series of paper cuts. But she was undaunted. There was a solution in there. She just needed more time to solve it.

Mercy General just needed better organization and a little less red tape. Too bad red was the favored color of the government. Madison had grown up playing with red tape. She knew where to cut and when. She knew ways around, above, and through. She could be of use here. She knew it.

Alongside notes on patient charts, she drafted a proposal for a new intake system and chart management. She looked over the budget and saw places to cut and expand.

By the time she was done, the sun had set. She hadn't seen a single patient, but she felt like she had touched them all. Her eyes were bleary from going over all that ink, and her mind was full of numbers. She needed a break, preferably an eight-hour break. Her two-star mattress back at the hotel was looking good right about now.

"Dr. Gray?" one of the nurses called to her on her way out. "Major Hanson was asking for you."

"Major Hanson?"

The moment Madison said his name, the image of

his handsome face bloomed in her mind, shoving away all the numbers and other names. Which was odd for her because she always remembered a patient's chart before she could recall their faces. That was what was most important; the data about what was happening inside, not their outside appearance.

Maybe she was just remembering this patient's face because of the importance he meant to her career. If she could convince him to get the surgery that she was certain he needed, that would hold a lot of sway with Chief Pena and her winning the Chief of Orthopedic Surgery position that she'd come here for in the first place.

Madison took the chart the nurse handed her and went down to his floor. When she came up to Major Hanson's room, she noted a group of people walking away from the door. They were a colorful and eclectic bunch, reminding her of her friends back in New York.

Not that she got to seen her friends a lot during her five-year surgical internship. She'd seen even less of them during her two-year residency. In fact, she wasn't sure she had most of their numbers any longer since many had gotten married or moved. She hadn't even had a going away party when she's left New York, just a few social media posts that were met with hearts and confetti emojis.

The group in Major Hanson's doorway looked like they were as thick as thieves and stuck together like glue. They probably left words on social media posts and not just a series of emojis. In fact, not a single phone was out. They blew kisses with fingers against lips, said goodbye with their actual mouths and waves of hands. With that much hand action, Madison doubted they would ever lose touch.

"Dr. Gray, you're finally here."

Madison recognized the brown-eyed man from earlier. He'd been the one to give the initial run down on Major Hanson's condition. His expression was pinched as he looked down his nose at her, as though he was the parent of a child she'd just given a bad grade to.

"Dr. Lamb was here earlier. He said he didn't think Paul needed surgery, but he wanted to run more tests."

Madison pursed her lips at the mention of Doug. He said he would play fair, but here he was already overstepping his bounds. They'd agreed to run more tests and then present their findings to Pena. But, of course, Doug ignored the rules so he could get himself front and center.

Seriously, what had she ever seen in the man?

"Paul says he wanted to hear from you before making any decisions since you are his doctor. But I think he's just stalling. He's not a fan of surgery. The first one… and now this. Do you really think he needs surgery?"

"I can't discuss that with you," said Madison.

"I have power of attorney."

Madison looked the man over again. Had she misread Major Hanson's flirting the other day? This guy had been hovering over him like a nagging wife. And then she remembered Major Hanson's eye-rolling retort from the other day.

"Oh? Now I get why he called you mom," said Madison.

A bark of laughter came from the room. It was full and deep-bellied. The sound wrapped around her, inviting her to come inside and play.

"Marry me," Major Hanson said when she went inside the room. "But, first, shut the door, so mom won't walk in on us."

Madison did as her patient asked. She shut out the male helicopter mom, who did not look at all amused. Well, there was no need for a power of attorney, as the patient was in possession of his full mental faculties. Though that impromptu marriage proposal gave Madison pause.

"Any woman—aside from his wife—who can shut Luke down like that deserves my undying devotion."

"He cares about you," she said. She watched as Luke's friends tugged him down the hall toward the exit. Most people would've been thrilled to have such a large group of people surrounding and cheering for their recovery.

"He blames himself for this." Major Hanson waved his hand up and down his prone body.

Madison looked Major Paul Hanson up and down. He looked every bit a virile man. A handsome, virile man. A handsome, virile man who knew it. As evidenced by the smirk on his face.

"You wanted to talk about your condition, Major Hanson?"

"Call me Paul."

"You didn't like your second opinion, *Major Hanson?*"

"That guy seems like an idiot."

A litany of every wrong Doug had committed against her during their relationship came to mind. But then, so did the truth. "No," she huffed the word. "He's not an idiot. He's brilliant, actually."

"Any man who would let a woman like you slip through his fingers is an idiot."

For the first time in her life as a medical professional, Madison blushed. She was alone in a room with a man reclining on a bed in nothing more than a slip of thin fabric. Major Hanson did not look like an invalid. He looked like a warrior having a rest before he went back to the business of conquering.

Madison gave her head a shake and looked down at his chart. "Your condition is serious, Major. My instinct tells me it may be a pinched nerve, but I need to do more tests."

"You trust your instincts?"

"After I back them up with data, always."

"I don't believe that." He shook his head. "I think your gut tells you the right answer. The data is so that other people will believe you."

"Do you want me to just cut you open blind and poke around to feel for the right answer?"

He grinned like a lion toying with a mouse. He was mistaken to think of her as something so small. At the least, Madison was a gazelle, and she was going to outrun this predator.

She opened her mouth to cut him down to size. Only she didn't feel in the least threatened by him. She didn't feel leered at or patronized. Major

Hanson's gaze stayed strictly north, right on her eyes. Like he liked sparring with her, talking to her, seeing what she'd say next.

He'd asked her to marry him a moment ago. Sure, it had been a joke. But still, it had made her tingle.

"Let me help you, Paul."

His breath caught at the use of his name. His gaze dipped then. Down to his legs, not hers.

"My gut says you need surgery. I want to be sure exactly what kind so that I give you exactly what you need."

His gaze lifted and met hers. Madison had to resist the urge to gulp. His eyes were so wide, so open that she would've sworn she could see right into the heart of him.

Which was impossible. If she saw right into his eyes, she'd see first his ocular nerve, followed by brain matter. Not his heart.

"I'll let you run some tests," he said finally. "But I'm not agreeing to another surgery. Not yet."

"Deal." She held out her hand.

He took it. And when he did, electricity sparked across her wrist. Madison's breath caught then. She couldn't catch it in time to silence it.

That lion-like smile spread even wider across his

handsome face. She'd thought she was fast, but she was a gazelle caught inside a lion's paw. And then he let her go.

Madison felt her legs wobble as she turned on her heel. Even when she walked out of the room, she felt as though he was following her. Which was impossible, as he was confined to the bed.

CHAPTER SEVEN

here was a chill in the air of the exam room. Off and on, Paul felt something nip at his toes. Those sensations were there and gone before he could be sure. Playing peekaboo like the rest of him was a child. But unlike a baby, Paul was never surprised when the feeling came back to his legs. He knew that each time his nerves hid his sense of touch away that it would always come back to reveal itself.

He was happy to wait awhile longer for the sensations to come home and stay for good so long as he was able to keep looking at Madison Gray. The gorgeous doctor kept hiding behind the clipboard with his medical records or dipping behind the machine. Each time she returned, Paul felt a giddy bubble of joy in his chest, like a baby seeing the magic of what was once lost unveiled again.

Paul wanted to turn and twist his body so that she was always within view. But he lay prone at the mouth of an MRI machine. The large oven-looking machine waited to eat his body whole.

"Now, you just relax, Major," said the nurse as she patted his leg.

Paul couldn't feel her tapping. He could only see the actions. Her smile was comforting, like his grandmother's. Her midwestern twang was oddly maternal.

"This is why I keep coming back here," he said. "The hospitality is better than a five-star hotel."

The nurse—Reeves was her surname. Nurse Reeves giggled, just like his grandmother.

A throat cleared on the far side of the room. "If you two are done flirting, we need to get this procedure started."

Dr. Madison Gray spoke with pursed lips. Her hazel gaze was on the clipboard in her hand, not on either Paul or Nurse Reeves. Madison thought they were flirting? As though Paul could pay attention to anyone else when she was in the room.

Paul couldn't tell if the doctor was joking or not? He expected not with the pinch to her beautiful features. Just the fact that she'd used the term flirting made Paul wonder if she was in any way jealous. Which then made him wonder if maybe he had a real shot at taking her out on a date?

"I'll leave you in Dr. Gray's hands," said the nurse as she headed for the door to the lab.

"I couldn't ask for better in my wildest dreams," said Paul.

Madison looked up from the clipboard then. There was surprise on her beautiful face. Her long lashes fluttered like they were butterfly wings. Her heart-shaped lips rounded into a soft O.

At that moment, Paul would've given up the use of his legs to pull her close. He didn't need his feet or his knees to taste that letter of the alphabet on her lips. Just his hands and mouth. Anything else was dead weight.

But she turned away from him, hiding her features. By the time she turned back around, the O was gone, and her gaze was narrowed.

"So, Major Hanson, the MRI machine is basically a big, 3-D x-ray machine. It will draw images of the deep tissue and skeletal system of your body, which will allow me to get a clearer picture of what's gone wrong with you."

"I know the drill, Maddie. It's not my first rodeo. And there's nothing wrong with me. Just a setback."

Her head whipped to him. Hazel eyes burning bright. For a moment, Paul was mesmerized. Whatever just happened to bring that look onto her face, he wanted to do it again.

"What did you just say?"

Paul couldn't remember what he'd said? He couldn't see anything past that golden spark in her eyes. He'd said something about a drill and a rodeo. That was all.

Oh, wait? Maddie. He'd called her Maddie.

"Did I overstep?" he asked.

Madison swallowed. "My mother used to call me Maddie."

She said it with that far-off look that let him know that her mother was in heaven and not here with them.

"It suits you," he said. "Part girly. Part fierce warrior."

"I'm neither girly nor a warrior." She snorted. Then caught herself, and the professional look was back.

"I think those shoes would beg to differ."

Today, she wore a pair of six-inch heels. They did wonders to accentuate her lean calf muscles.

"They were my mother's shoes. She was a beauty queen. She left me all her clothes, shoes, and handbags."

A soft expression came across her face. Paul said nothing as she got lost in her memories. It gave him a reason to bask in the beauty of her. He could imagine Madison being from pageantry stock.

"Anyway," she said, clearing her throat and looking back at her clipboard. "We should get you started. The sooner we find answers, the sooner I'll know how to fix you."

"I already told you, Dr. Gray, there's nothing wrong with me."

She studied him then. Really peering down at him with those bright eyes. "A man like you should be on his feet and not on his back."

"I don't mind so much when I have this view of looking up at you."

She inhaled. Not in the quick way of someone who was shocked. Her intake of breath was slow and controlled, as though she was tempering the words she was about to say.

"You're going to have to stop with this flirting. I'm your doctor, and your condition is serious."

"Dr. Vader doesn't think I need surgery at all."

"Dr. Vader?"

"The idiot you dumped. He's clearly been seduced by the dark side of the force."

Madison snorted. A full opened mouth snort where her nostrils flared and the sound caught in her throat. Paul found it delightful.

"So what? You're Han Solo. Your helicopter mom is Luke Skywalker. Doug is Darth Vader. And I'm …" She raised those brows at him. The O reforming on her lips. "Am I Princess Leia?"

"You seemed too serious to be a princess. You know Leia grew up to become a general. I think that suits you."

"Stop flirting with me." But she was struggling to hide a grin as she said it.

"I can't help it. Not now when Nurse Reeves has left me."

Madison tried to stop the smile from coming to her lips. She failed.

"You can always run away if you don't like it, Maddie."

"What I'm going to do is make your legs better so that you can return to soldiering for the Rebel Alliance."

That elicited a laugh from Paul. Women didn't always get his Star Wars references. Just another sign that Madison was different.

"I'm very good at what I do, Paul. Trust me."

Madison placed her hand on his knee. When she did, the grin fell from Paul's face. He could feel her hand. He could feel his toes. He wiggled the toes of one foot. Then the other. He bent his knee up, which displaced her hand.

Madison looked down at his legs in shock. She stepped back in disbelief when Paul sat up and swung his legs around and off the table.

"Wait," said Madison. "I don't think you should-"

But Paul was already doing it. He was standing. Standing tall, without any pain in either of his legs.

CHAPTER EIGHT

Madison's clipboard clattered to the floor. She didn't bother to reach for it. She was prepared to catch Paul if he fell.

Though how she would manage that, she had no idea. She'd only seen the man sitting or lying prone in a bed. She had no idea just how tall he was. He stood well over six feet, towering over her even in her high heels.

Neither had she been prepared for just how broad he was. Unlike the hotel bed she'd slept in last night, she could fit her whole body against Major Paul Hanson's chest and still have room to toss and turn. The man was a California king size bed. Which meant that if he did fall, her twin-sized body would be crushed.

So why didn't that thought make her move out of his way?

Maybe because she had never felt both dwarfed by and secure in front of a man before? Maybe because she had been wanting to take a break and curl up on his form even when he'd been laying prone in the hospital bed? Maybe because she got the sense that he wasn't the one that was falling. It was her.

But Major Paul Hanson didn't fall. He stood on strong, sturdy legs. His bare toes rooted into the ground to allow the rest o him to spring up and tower over the MRI machine.

It should not be possible for him to stand in his condition. And yet, there he was. Standing tall with the proudest, cheekiest grin on that handsome face of his. He didn't wobble. He didn't falter.

Paul Hanson stood like a mountain that Madison could take shelter in. Which was funny, because Madison had never been the kind of woman to seek shelter from a man. She was the kind of woman who booked the poshest cabin at the top of the mountain and glamped in warmth and luxury.

Just looking at Paul standing tall before her and she knew he was the kind of man who could build her that cabin. He was the kind of man who would carry her up to it. He was the kind of man who would keep her warm for the rest of the days.

Madison gave her head a shake. What was she thinking? This was a patient. A patient who just might be a medical miracle.

If she was smart, and she had been at the top of her class, she would be documenting this; a man who presented with degenerative spinal disease but was now standing. She should be looking at the chart, taking notes, asking questions.

Instead, she said, "You need to sit down."

"I've been sitting for two days," said Paul, still towering over her like a mighty lion.

Only now that he was on two legs, he made her think of a bear. Though there was still a rumbly purr to his voice. But deeper. Almost like a growl. Had his voice grown deeper? Or was it just that his words were now sailing down toward her instead of rising up?

"It feels good to stretch my legs," he said, straightening his spine to rise another inch. He put his shoulders back and blocked out the rest of the room.

Madison gazed up at him. He grinned down at her.

Her hand rose to his chest. She felt his strong

heartbeat beneath her fingers. Her hand had had a purpose in rising to his chest. What had it been?

Oh, right. She had meant to give him a push to get him sitting again. But it seemed there was a magnet inside his chest. Once her fingers brushed the thin cotton there, she couldn't seem to let go. That drum beat of his heart reverberated all through her.

"This shouldn't be possible," she said.

She wasn't sure if she was referring to him standing? Or if she was referring to the powerful attraction that had sprung up between them.

"Why not? You said you have magic hands." Paul's hand covered hers. "Maybe that's what healed me."

"You're not healed."

But was he? Had she been wrong about his diagnosis? It was possible that his body might work out the kinks of his initial injury. But she hadn't been prepared to bet on those chances. Mainly because Madison wasn't a betting woman. She preferred facts over odds.

Paul's hand reached up to cover his large paw with hers. Again, she had never felt so delicate with another living soul. That desire to snuggle into the center of his chest came over again. He was just a few inches away. She could rest there and regain her senses. It looked like he wouldn't mind. Not with how he was smiling down at her like she was a flower filled with honey.

His thumb reached up and brushed the bottom of her chin. A shiver went through Madison. That sensation was followed by a liquid warmth that spread up her elbows and across her shoulder blades, like golden honey running all the way through her.

Yeah. She could take just a moment to rest there. Just sit back and relax in the hold of this big bear of a man who would likely growl at anything that came near his stash of honey. And she was the honey.

"What's going on here?"

The sound of Doug's voice was like a nightmare in the middle of a dream. Madison peered around Paul's massive shoulders to see her ex standing in the lab's open door. Doug's gaze was locked on Madison's hand, which was still against Paul's pounding heart.

Madison noted that she was staring Doug right in his eyes. Because he never towered over her. He was on her level. She had an inch on him when she wore her heels, which she'd stopped doing as much when they'd dated. Which was a shame since flats simply didn't become her long legs. She'd started wearing them again after they'd broken up.

However, her shoes weren't the issue at the moment. The issue was that she was standing in the embrace of a patient.

No. No, that wasn't exactly the problem. The problem was that she was melting into the embrace of a patient.

Yes, that was it. Because if Paul had simply made a pass at her, she could've handled it herself. Paul had made a pass, and Madison was standing firm inside his catch.

Or she had been. Paul was shrinking down to her size. No, he wasn't shrinking. He was collapsing.

"Major Hanson? Paul!"

His features contorted into horror as his massive chest caved in. He released his gentle hold on her face and grasped for the bed, but not quickly enough. With his legs slowly giving out, there was nothing for him to balance on. Madison was not strong enough to hold all of his weight. Just as she had predicted, his large bulk was going to crush her.

CHAPTER NINE

One moment Paul had been standing tall in front of Madison. He'd felt the urge to pick her up, sweep her off her feet, and carry her away from this hospital to a field of flowers, just like in some sappy romance movie. The next, he was falling into her, his own legs knocked out from under him.

He'd like to say his pride had been hurt from that fall. The truth was that Paul felt nothing as his body came crashing down around Madison. At least he'd had the presence of mind to twist his torso to avoid direct impact.

It was just too bad that Dr. Lamb hadn't made it over in time. Paul would've happily crash-landed on top of the man. But no, Lamb had stood dumbfounded in the doorway, not moving until after Madison was tugging at Paul's forearms in vain.

It had taken Madison and the MRI technician to get him back onto the table. In the end, the medical professionals decided it was best to have him go into the machine to get the details that they needed to figure out what was going on with his body.

Paul was thankful for the solitude inside the machine. The machine clanked loudly, making him feel he was inside a clock tower with rusty gears. He was even more thankful that he had no choice but to keep still as the machine began its detective work to figure out what was wrong with him.

Paul knew exactly what was wrong with him. He'd gotten cocky. And just like the mighty Sampson, who allowed his vanity to get the better of him, he'd allowed his growing feelings for a woman to weaken him. Well, at least Paul still had his hair. So there was a bright side.

"Just a few minutes more, Major Hanson."

The sound of Madison's sweet voice filled with professionalism grated on Paul's nerves. She'd called him Paul twenty minutes ago. He'd been getting under her skin. He'd been close enough to kiss her. When he'd stood over her, she hadn't pulled away. She'd tilted up her head like an invitation.

Paul hated that he'd had to decline. He wanted a rain check, and he wanted it now. The only place he'd get to taste the sweetness of her lips was in his dreams. Paul closed his eyes and tuned out the world.

Even behind his closed lids, he was seeing a dream. He saw a woman walking to him, barefoot in a field. Her golden-brown skin in stark contrast to the green blades of grass. In his mind, his gaze panned up to a pastel-colored dress covering a round belly filled with a child, his child.

"Major Hanson?"

Paul had to get to the woman of his dreams. But he was encased inside a tomb. The truth was, the real tomb was his body. One day it would work and the next it wouldn't. If he didn't get answers, he would not only be out of a job, he had no idea how he'd live his life.

"Paul?"

Paul opened his eyes. The fluorescent lights overhead urged his lids to close, but he couldn't. He didn't dare. His dream come true stood over him.

"I'm going to marry you," he said.

Madison's lips parted. He watched her try and fail and then try again to swallow. She tried to pull the professional veneer back over herself. It was a joy to watch. But he wasn't fooled. He saw right through her.

"I had a vision," he said.

"Oh?" She frowned. "You had a vision while inside an MRI machine?"

"Clear as day. Though you were smiling in my vision. Made you look a lot prettier."

"I think maybe we need that psych consult after all." But there was a smile in her words that didn't quite stretch across her mouth.

"That might be for the best since I see those little hearts and tweety birds floating around again."

That was a definite smile on her face. "I'll schedule an optometry consult as well."

"You should probably add cardiology onto that, too. My heart keeps skipping beats when you're near."

The war between professional and woman was lost. Madison grinned like a schoolgirl at the after-school dance. And even though he lay prone on a medical table, Paul felt like he could take on the world for this woman.

A throat cleared behind them. The sound was louder than the churning gears of the MRI machine. Madison looked over her shoulder, and the gates of her features clanged down in place.

"If the two of you are done flirting," said Dr. Lamb, "we have results to look at."

Madison pulled her clipboard to her chest like it was armor. Paul noted she had an inch over Dr. Lamb. It appeared Dr. Lamb noted it as well. He looked down at Madison's heels with irritation.

Paul used his forearms to push himself up to a sitting position. His legs were still number and useless. But from his seated position, Paul was eye to eye with the other man.

"The tech will help you back to your room, Mr. Hanson," said Dr. Lamb.

"It's *Major* Hanson," Madison corrected.

Lamb ignored her. "While Dr. Gray and I discuss your results and consult with you later."

It was clear Lamb meant his terse words to be a dismissal. He turned on his heel, his over-polished shoes squeaking on the linoleum. He paused when he got to the door, turning back for Madison.

"I'll be there in a second," she said.

Lamb glared at her. His eyes shouting protests that even Paul could hear. With a slight raise of Madison's brow, Lamb lost the staring contest. He huffed out a breath and walked out the door.

Madison turned back to Paul. There was worry in the crease of her brow. Paul wanted to reach up and smooth it away. Instead, he kept his hands to himself.

"You've seen the results?" he said.

She canted her head to the side like a bird. She scratched at her chest with the other hand not holding the clipboard. All while avoiding his gaze.

"It's bad?"

"I want to take a closer look before I make any determinations."

She wasn't telling him everything. She wasn't telling him anything. Instead of fear or trepidation, Paul felt calm and certainty. Just as he knew he would heal and walk again, he knew that the vision he'd seen of Madison in the field was true.

Call it faith. Call it crazy. It was going to happen.

"Promise me something?" he said.

Madison shuffled uncomfortably.

"If it's surgery, I want you to do it."

Her gaze did meet his then. Her palm flattened on her chest. She took a step closer to him.

"And if it's a success, you'll go on a date with me after."

She took a step back. "I cannot promise that. It's against ethics."

"For you to heal me? Didn't you take an oath? Or are you a hypocrite?"

That earned another crack of a smile from her. "It's a Hippocratic Oath. The doctor dating a patient thing is against hospital policy."

"I respect that. But after the surgery, you won't be my doctor anymore, so that won't be a problem. Unless you don't think you can actually heal me."

"You're incorrigible, you know that."

"A man won't get far without a little courage."

Madison took two steps toward him. She was standing so close that the fabric of her white coat brushed up against his knees. Even though he couldn't feel anything below his waist, he still felt warmth flood his chest.

"Paul, I promise you one thing, I'm going to do everything I can to get you back on your feet. Mainly, because it's the only way I'll get you out of my hair."

And with that last quip, she turned and sauntered out of the room. Paul felt a tingle in his toes, watching her depart.

CHAPTER TEN

The door to the MRI lab room shut behind Madison with a quiet snick. Inside her head, there was a loud whoosh, like water cascading down from a waterfall. Or the beads of a hot shower falling down her back because Madison felt like she'd stepped under a warm spray after Paul's words.

Little read hearts? Tweety birds? Skipped beats.

Madison grinned at the memory. She tugged at her bottom lip with her teeth, trying to hold back the grin spreading there. She brushed a tendril of hair out of her face like she was at a bar and trying to signal the cute guy to come over and buy her a drink.

How did that man have this kind of effect on her?

He certainly wasn't the first patient to ever hit on her. But Madison had always easily shut the others down. The problem was, she liked sparring with Paul Hanson.

It never felt like he was coming on to her. Each time he flirted with her, by the time he'd stopped talking and it was her turn to respond with a witty quip, he had already snuck past her defenses. And Madison liked having him in enemy territory.

She'd worried he wouldn't try to sneak over her boundary line again after he'd collapsed at her feet. He'd shut down when he'd gone into the MRI machine. But he rallied shortly after coming out and had her smiling again. She'd almost giggled at his last advances like a smitten schoolgirl.

It was insane to think about going on a date with him. But in her head, she was already picking out her best outfit and a matching pair of stilettos because—if she had anything to do with it—Major Paul Hanson was going to stand tall again.

At least, she hoped he would. The initial results from the MRI did not look good. But Madison had been faced with worse charts. She was determined to figure out what was happening to his body and fix it.

"Exactly what do you think you're doing?"

The sound of Doug's voice wiped the smile from Madison's face. He stood at the edge of the hall. His feet planted in a wide stance. His fists balled and resting on his hips. His features pinched as though he'd just taken a whiff of antiseptic.

"I don't know what you're talking about," said Madison.

"You know exactly what I'm talking about. Wanna know how I know? You got an A in ethics class."

"While you got a B."

"That's exactly my point."

Madison planted her feet in a wide stance, mirroring Doug's posture. Instead of balling her fists and resting them on her hips, she crossed her arms over her chest and waited for his next missive.

"Are you trying to convince that patient to let you do the surgery over me?"

"What?" Madison dropped her arms to her sides. "Are you serious?"

"You've never used your feminine wiles before to get ahead."

"My feminine what!"

"You've always used your brain."

Madison wondered if she needed to go see psych or the eye doctor for herself. Those hearts that Paul had said he'd seen all around her burst now as she glared at her ex-boyfriend. All she could see was red.

"If you're trying to make me jealous, Madison, this isn't the way."

"Jealous? Why would I care about your feelings when there is no us?"

Doug's arms came to his sides, but his hands remained balled into fists. They stood eye to eye. But when Madison straightened her shoulders, she had an inch on him. She realized she'd always hunched a bit when they were dating. She put her shoulders back now and reveled in that breadth of height she had over him.

"You saw the scan. You know what it means."

Madison's shoulders slumped. She had seen the preliminary results. But she wasn't ready to admit the prognosis.

"He's failed all conservative non-surgical treatments," Doug began to list off Paul's issues. "His microdiscectomy failed. And the MRI showed that the impacted disc is severely degenerated with endplate erosion."

Madison wanted to close her eyes to all the

evidence that had been in black and white. What it all meant was surgery. A very serious procedure that she would've been chomping at the bit to dig her scalpel into on any other day, in any other patient.

"I get it. You're just pitying him," said Doug.

"Pity? There's nothing about that man to pity. He's a hero."

"He's a broken soldier, Madison. We're going to see a lot of them while here. We won't be able to fix all of them. He might be one of the unfixable."

Madison looked at Doug anew. She didn't believe for a second that Paul was unfixable, not with the strength he displayed while laying prone in a bed. The man who was unfixable, unsalvageable, was the one facing her.

"Doug, what exactly are you doing here if you don't think we can help these patients?"

He shrugged as though the question was inane. "This is just part of the overall plan. It's going to look great on my resume that I worked for a VA hospital when we finally move back to the city. It won't matter which one of us gets the chief position, not when we're a power surgical team. Any major hospital will be salivating to have us."

The red drained from her vision, and she saw Doug clearly. He was still playing the game. Still competing with her like they'd done all throughout their studies. But Madison wasn't in school anymore. This was her real life.

"You're right, Doug. This was always my plan. But what you don't understand is that this is my end goal. Working at a veterans' hospital isn't some jumping-off point for me. It's where I want to be."

Doug huffed an annoyed breath. "Fine, we can stay for a couple of years. But we're going back to civilization when we start our family."

"For the last time, there is no us."

"You know those other women meant nothing, Madison. I have plans to spend my life with you."

Madison could only shake her head as she regarded this man she wasted so much time on.

"Look, I won't tell the chief about your little indiscretion with a patient."

In her mind, Madison heard shots fired. She felt the enemy encroaching on her territory. She sucked in a slow, deep breath, pulling on her armor.

"There's nothing to tell," she said.

"Then have dinner with me."

Proximity alarms blared all around her. Danger and warning signs flashed yellow and red. "No. Because I don't want to. Not as your girlfriend. Not as your colleague. I'm not even sure I want to be your friend right now."

And with that, she walked off down the hall. Heels clacking like boots in a forward march. Thankfully, she didn't hear the squeak of Doug's expensive shoes following her.

CHAPTER ELEVEN

Paul was still reeling from Dr. Lamb's interruption. It was the second time he'd been in kissing distance of Madison, and the man had stepped in and blocked him. The dark side of the force was really trying to get at him today.

Interestingly enough, Paul had been virtually helpless each time he was near enough to Madison to steal a kiss. But somehow, helpless was the last thing he felt when he was close to that woman.

Madison's touch brought Paul back to life. Her smile made him feel as though he could conquer an advancing army of insurgents. What was wrong with him—whatever it was—he knew it was temporary. Just an annoying blip on his way to a life with Madison Gray.

One day soon, he'd stand tall and sweep her off her feet. He felt it in his bones. His toes tingled with certainty.

Except now, he was rolling away from her. Leaving her behind with that Vader in designer suit clothing.

"You look like a soldier preparing for battle."

Paul glanced up to see Dr. Patel coming down the hall. The Purple Heart Ranch's resident psychologist wore his usual amused grin. Paul hadn't put much stock in psychology. But when the doctor, who was also a pastor, mixed in scripture with his head shrinking, Paul became a convert of Patel's ways. He was the first person to suggest that Paul take up riding when he came to the ranch.

Dr. Patel had been right in his assessment. It was the horses that had begun the process of putting Paul back together again. Paul itched to mount one of the majestic beasts and ride away from there. Preferably with a pretty surgeon in tow.

"I'll take over from here," Dr. Patel said to the technician who had been wheeling Paul back to his room. The tech happily released Paul into Patel's hold.

"Did Luke send you to check on me?" Paul asked as they began to roll down the hall toward his room.

"I was on rounds here at the hospital. I work with many of the soldiers here as well as on the ranch."

Paul frowned, wondering what Patel would prescribe for a soldier here at Mercy General? There wasn't a stable out back. Then Paul remembered Madison's threat to get him a psych evaluation.

"Was it Madison who sent you?"

"Madison? You mean the new surgeon, Dr. Gray?"

"Yes, her."

Paul couldn't see Dr. Patel's face, but he was sure the old man was grinning. From what he'd been told when he'd come to Purple Heart Ranch, Dr. Patel had had a hand in matchmaking most of the couples there. Marriages of convenience were another of the man's specialties.

"Madison—Dr. Gray—has been joking about me being crazy."

"Joking?" asked Patel.

"Because I told her I see stars and hearts and baby birds flying around when she's near."

It was the truth. But a truth from his imagination. He didn't actually see those things. What if she did think he was crazy? He'd have to set her straight. But what would he tell her instead? That he felt in his soul that they were meant to be together. Just as he felt it deep in his gut that he would stand on his own two feet again.

"Strong emotions can sometimes manifest as realistic visions," Dr. Patel was saying.

Paul should've known Dr. Patel wouldn't have chided him. He might be a doctor of the mind, but he was also a man of God. That meant he knew that sometimes truth wasn't always tangible.

"She's the one," Paul admitted. "I feel it in my bones all the way down to my toes."

"You do?" asked Dr. Patel. "Does that mean you'll get the surgery?"

Paul took a deep breath. When he'd first been injured, he knew that it was by divine mercy and a hovering best friend that he'd survived. With his faith and his strong body, he'd decided to leave his healing in the hands of a higher power.

Exercise, a good diet, and prayer had worked for months. Until the tingles and loss of sensation began. Then he'd succumbed to the demand for surgery.

And here he was doing worse than before. Except when Madison was around. When she was with him, Paul felt more than he'd ever felt in his life. The problem was she wanted to cut him open and rearrange him from the inside out.

"I've never understood how you, a man of God, can coexist in the world of science," said Paul.

"God gave his children the ability to learn to heal our bodies and the science of modern medicine."

"I was taught that faith heals."

"You have a picture in your mind of what your healing looks like. I believe this frustration comes when your plan of healing is different from His."

Paul was not a man who wrestled with his faith. He knew he was here for a purpose. He had felt called to serve his country in the military. After his injury, he felt a kinship with the horses who aided in his healing. Now, his heart cried out for a certain doctor whose hands felt like magic to his frayed nerves.

"Dr. Gray is at the top of her field," said Dr. Patel. "I believe your health is in good hands with her."

It wasn't his health that Paul was worried about. It was his heart. Another surgery could heal him or leave him worse off than he was now. But a man wasn't a man without his heart, and Paul's heart was ready to jump the ship of his chest to be with Madison.

What if she wasn't prepared to catch it? What if

she healed his back and then had no further interest in him?

No. No, he didn't believe that was true. He'd seen the way she'd looked up at him in the MRI lab. She'd wanted him. She just didn't want to want him.

Maybe it was that Hippocratic oath. If she allowed herself to feel anything for him more than as a patient, it would make her work difficult. But just as Paul couldn't make his legs work at will right now, he couldn't tell his heart who to latch onto.

When they arrived at his hospital room, Paul saw the figure of a woman moving about inside. His heart leaped that it might be Madison. A pale-skinned woman with coffee-colored eyes turned and smiled at him.

"Yes, Luke sent me. No, he's not here. But I brought entertainment."

Paul's heart thudded to the bottom of his chest. But it quickly rallied when Elaine held up his box of board games. He'd been bored to tears during his stay, with nothing to do but wait for glimpses of Madison.

"I'm glad you're here, Elaine. If my best friend hadn't scooped you up, I would've married you."

"So you propose to women a lot, I see," Madison

said as she walked toward him. Those hazel eyes sparkling like the sun's rays touching down on sand.

Paul heard the chirp of a bird outside. His gaze fixed on the red of her lips. And his heart skipped over its ventricles, and it shoved at the front of his chest to get to her.

CHAPTER TWELVE

"Is this her?" said the pretty woman with her hand on Paul's shoulder.

She wasn't the type Madison would've thought Paul would choose. She looked like a librarian with her pastel cardigan and white blouse. But she had a warm smile, like that guy on public television who invited kids to take a look in a book and go on a reading rainbow.

Paul wasn't looking at the woman or her smile. He was gazing at Madison with a goofy look on his face that reminded Madison of—well, Goofy, the cartoon dog when he saw Clarabelle, the cow. The same goofy look from the first time they'd met when he'd threatened to crawl to the intake desk.

The same goofy look when he'd asked her to marry him.

Just like he'd asked this woman to marry him.

"Don't let me interrupt your second proposal of the day," said Madison.

There was a chuckle that came from the corner of the room. Madison looked over to see one of the psychologists on staff. She'd only met Dr. Patel once, but she'd liked him instantly. He winked at her as he turned and walked out of the room.

So it looked like Paul had had the psych consult. Maybe this was his condition. He chronically asked women to marry him.

"This is her," Paul was saying to the other woman. He leaned in close to her, stage-whispering in her ear. "This is my future wife, Dr. Madison Gray."

How could Paul be referring to Madison as his future wife in front of the woman he was currently proposing to?

"She's pretty," said his other future wife.

"No, she's not. She's breathtaking. She swept me right off my feet. Literally, made my legs go out from under me when I looked into her eyes."

Warning signs were flaring up all around Madison. Not the black and yellow danger signs. These were the blaring red lights of a proximity alert. The problem was that the intruder was already in the house.

Here again, Paul had slipped past her defenses before she'd even known she was under attack. Madison didn't feel the need to slip on any armor. In fact, she wanted out of her white coat and heels. She wanted to curl up beside Paul and let all her worries melt away in his strong hold.

"If she can get you back on your feet, then Luke will approve," said the other woman.

"She's right, Maddie." Paul sighed. "We can't get married without Luke's approval."

"Who's Luke?" asked Madison.

"My mom," said Paul.

"My husband," said the woman, giving Paul a slap on the shoulder. She slapped Paul with her left hand, where a diamond sparkled on her fourth finger.

"Ouch, Elaine. I'm a wounded man in his sickbed."

"Hi, Dr. Gray. I'm Elaine. I work at the town library. Have you gotten your library card yet?"

"I… no," said Madison, looking between the two. "I haven't even found a place to live yet. I'm still in a hotel."

So Elaine wasn't going to marry Paul. Not that

Madison cared. She wasn't going to marry Paul, either.

"This works perfect," said Paul. "I just got a new place. You can move in with me. After we're married, of course."

"Right," said Madison, her head spinning from the onslaught that was Major Paul Hanson. His offensives were coming from every direction and making her dizzy. "Elaine, can I talk to my fiancé—I mean my patient—alone?"

Paul's goofy grin spread impossibly wider. But after Elaine left, he took one look at Madison's grim expression, and he sobered.

"You have my MRI results," said Paul.

Madison nodded.

"You don't like what you found."

"You're going to need surgery," Madison said.

Paul hefted himself out of the wheelchair and onto the bed as Madison went over his test results and her diagnosis. "Spinal fusion," he repeated the type of surgery she'd said he'd need.

Madison came to stand beside him. She wanted to reach out to touch him, partly to reassure him but somewhat to reassure herself as well. "I'm good at what I do, Paul. I'm the best."

"I believe you," he said.

He said it simply. Not a flinch. Not a hesitation.

He said it with a certainty she didn't know was possible. When he said it, she knew it was the truth. She was going to heal this man. He would stand again. But his belief in her ability wasn't a yes to the surgery.

"Is that a yes?" she asked.

Paul grinned. Not the wide, goofy grin. This one was more subdued, a little tired. "I'll tell you what, I'll play you for it."

He reached off to the side of the bed and into a packing box. Out of the box, he pulled a child's game.

"This is your health. Your life. It's not some game."

"What? You think you'll lose?"

Madison blew a gust of air out of her nose. How did this man tweak her confidence and her competitiveness at the same time?

"What I want, Dr. Gray, is a few moments with you while I'm whole and conscious before you have me on my back."

"It's back surgery. You'd be laying on your front."

His grin spread wider, nearing goofy size. "Are you so eager to cut me open?"

"I make beautiful scars, you know." Madison

pulled up a chair to the edge of his bead. "I'm going to kick your butt in this game."

"I believe that too," said Paul. "But here's the thing; if you win this game, you get your surgery. If you get your surgery, you'll heal me. If I'm healed, I get a date. So there's no way I can lose."

CHAPTER THIRTEEN

After winning the first game and losing the second, Paul knew three things about Dr. Madison Gray.

The first thing Paul knew about the woman was that she bit her lip when she was deep in thought. She nibbled at the left side when she was uncertain and was still working through her thoughts. She clamped down on the right side of her lip when she'd solved the problem and was sure she'd backed her opponent into a corner.

Paul settled back against the pillows on his hospital bed. He crossed his arms over his chest and watched the show at play on Madison's mouth. Her lips were pursed together now as she studied the game board.

But, no, wait. Just there. He saw it.

The pearly white of her left incisor snuck out. The sharp point bit down into the plump flesh on the left side of her mouth in uncertainty. Everything in Paul ached to reach his thumb out and tug at her lower lip, to wipe away the uncertainty and replace it with a kiss.

The flash of white disappeared. Madison retracted her left tooth, but it left a dent. A grin split her beautiful face, and her right incisor bit down on the right side of her mouth.

So she thought she had him. She was right. Madison had Paul completely at her mercy.

The grooves of the ridged game pieces made a grinding noise as Madison pressed them together in a windshield-wiping motion between her thumb and forefinger. It should've grated on Paul's nerves. But, like everything about this woman, he found the sound delightful.

Madison reached out and dropped a red game piece into a slot at the top of the yellow chute. The plastic slid down the grid and landed with a thud on top of one of his black pieces that had gone down the chute a few moments ago.

"Your move, Major."

Paul didn't bother looking down at the standing

game board. He simply raised his hands and let one of his black pieces drop down the chute and land where it may. The move elicited the exact response he'd been after.

"What? Are you insane?" Madison huffed. "Why would you make that move when you could've blocked me?"

Paul tore his gaze from the cute scrunch of Madison's face to look down at the game. He hadn't played Connect Four since he was a kid. But that was the game at the top of the box. It could've been Candy Land for all he cared. Because it wasn't about the game. It was simply about playing. That might have been what was happening with him. It was a different story with Madison.

The second thing Paul knew about Madison was that she was competitive. She went into the arena expecting to win. And she did not like to lose.

Even in something as trivial as a kid's game, Madison had gone in with a strategy. The first round of the game, she had played the middle column, aiming to gain a strategic advantage and push him to the edge. She was pushing him to the edge, all right. Little did she know that Paul was one to push back, but she was about to find out.

As Madison became focused on taking control,

Paul easily snuck past her defenses and built a solid diagonal line that she'd missed. Her lovely face had contorted in disbelief as she counted and then recounted the four black pieces that connected to give him the victory.

"Let's play again," she had demanded.

Paul had agreed. The second time they'd played, she'd won. Because the second time, Paul had been focused on learning and memorizing her facial features as she played. Which led him to the lip-biting discovery. His attentiveness to the lip-biting had led to his loss.

As a soldier, he knew that sometimes a battle had to be lost in order to make an advance. He'd gathered valuable intel with that loss. Even more valuable intel than when he'd watched her win.

The third and final thing Paul knew about Madison—and this he knew for certain—was that he was definitely going to win. Not the third game in the tiebreaker of their Connect Four bout. It didn't matter which of them connected four game pieces first. Paul was going to win at connecting the two of them together. Because unlike Madison, who was playing simply to win, Paul was playing for keeps.

Except when he looked down to make a new

move in the children's game, he realized he didn't have any pieces left. Neither did Madison. They'd packed the game board without making the appropriate amount of connections with their game pieces.

"A tie?" said Madison in utter disbelief. "I didn't even know that was possible in this game."

"Maybe you've finally met your match, Dr. Gray."

Madison bit at her lip. First, she nibbled at the left side with uncertainty. A second later, she tugged at the right. Finally, she tugged at the center to pull her whole bottom lip inside her mouth.

What did that mean?

"What does this mean?" she asked. "Does this mean you're going to let me perform the surgery?"

Oh, right. They were back to that. The game of life. His life.

Speaking of his life, Paul felt a twinge in his toes. He looked down at his leg. His torso was covered by a blanket, but he saw the twitch at the bottom edge of the covers.

Madison looked down as well. "You feel something?"

Once again with the loaded questions. "Yes. Yes, I do feel something."

Her gaze shifted from his legs to his face. Her

hand was on his knee, but she was leaning in to him. It would just take a few inches, and Paul would have that kiss he so desperately wanted.

He leaned forward.

Madison didn't retreat. She bit at the left side of her lip. Paul had every intention of placing his lips first on the left side of her mouth. He was going to wipe away any trace of uncertainty in this woman.

"Ahem." A throat cleared behind them.

The tingling in Paul's legs grew, letting him know that he had enough strength to stand. He was going to march over to the door and slam it in Dr. Vader's face.

"Chief!"

Before he could swing his legs off the bed, Madison leaped to standing. Her motion nearly sent the entire game board and its pieces scattering to the floor. But Paul caught it at the last second.

$\mathcal{M}$adison had had only one scolding in her entire life. The one and only time was from her father. Madison had gone to stay with her father's sister while he was away at an overnight event in Washington, DC. She'd begged him to go, promising she'd be on her best behavior. The General had been unmoved by her pleas, and Madison had been shipped off to Aunt Bess.

Aunt Bess was a tyrant who wouldn't let Madison do anything but sit still and keep quiet. When Madison decided she'd had enough of Aunt Bess's hospitality—which had been all of two hours into her stay—she decided she'd walk home. Over fifteen miles away. At the age of seven.

She'd been found three miles from Aunt Bess's,

walking on the side of the road. When her father had found out, he had been quiet at first. But after he had his daughter safe in her bedroom, he yelled so loud that the ceiling fan spun around even though the power switch was off.

Madison had sat quietly through the tirade. Though she'd been scared of her father's anger, she didn't budge from her belief that she'd been right in running away. Aunt Bess was the Wicked Witch come to life, and no child should be subjected to that. She'd never gone to spend the night again.

Madison sat in Chief Pena's office now. The man who had been her teacher, her mentor, and was now her boss sat quietly in his wingback chair. He was not even looking at her. He rubbed at the bridge of his nose. A red mark formed there from where his glasses sat all day. He took them off now and looked at her.

"Madison, you got an A on ethics," he began. "Though I wasn't your teacher, I know that to be true because you never got anything less than an A."

That wasn't true. There had been that B in Art History. She just couldn't bring herself to take Jackson Pollock seriously.

"There's nothing romantic going on between me and Major Hanson," said Madison.

The lie burned on Madison's tongue. Just a few moments ago, Madison had had the burning desire to press her lips against Paul's. There was absolutely no medical reason for her to do that.

"Romantic?" Chief Pena put his glasses back on. "I didn't say there was."

Madison pressed her back against the chair. Her chair didn't have a winged back, so there was no support for her shoulders. She wasn't sure which way this conversation was going? Part of her back was up because she thought she was being accused of inappropriate behavior with a patient, which there might be a smidge of truth to. The other part of her back was up because the chief hadn't seen anything romantic when he'd walked into the room.

Paul had wanted to kiss her. She was sure of it. He'd been staring at her lips all through the game. That's how he lost the first time. She had no idea how he'd won the second game. Or how they'd come to a stalemate in the third. What she did know was that she wanted a rematch. Not so much because she wanted to beat him. She just needed to know where she stood with him.

"I know that you know better than to get attached to your patients," the chief was saying. "You've never had that trouble before."

He was right. Madison had always looked at her patients as symptoms on a chart, a puzzle that she was going to solve. That's all Paul Hanson was. He was a scattered puzzle of symptoms. All of which were clues to help her to arrive at the right diagnosis and win this game.

"But you're clearly trying to one-up Doug so that you can get the Chief of Orthopedic Surgery position."

The position? Is that what he thought this was about?

Well, wasn't it about that?

Madison wanted the position. It's why she'd uprooted her whole life and moved out to the middle of nowhere. She wanted to help veterans like Paul. She wanted to solve their problems. The important problems of the women and men who gave so much to this country but often got the poorest health care.

"It looks like Major Hanson has agreed to do the surgery," said the chief.

He had? When? She'd only left him twenty minutes ago.

"I'll be the one deciding who is doing his surgery," said the chief.

Madison wanted to argue that point. She had

more surgeries under her belt than Doug. But only by a handful of operations.

Doug hadn't believed Paul even needed the surgery. He certainly wouldn't give Paul the care and detail to attention that she would. Madison would go in and find every little issue and solve it. She wouldn't cut corners like Doug had a tendency to do.

"No more trying to get Major Hanson to pick you to do the surgery," said the chief.

Madison pursed her lips together. She nodded. But she only agreed with the chief because Paul had agreed to the surgery only because of Madison. He'd been the one to pick her. Surely he would insist on Madison being his doctor. Just as he'd insisted on taking her out on a date after he was well. Just as he'd asked her to marry him more than once now. Madison realized she hadn't said no to either proposal.

She thought back to the time in the MRI room when he'd stood towering over her. She'd liked the feeling of him standing over her. She'd wanted to step into his broad chest, rest her head against his heart, and let all of her worries fall away.

She'd felt the same draw when they'd tied in Connect Four. Madison hated losing. Hated unclear outcomes even more. She wanted to go back to Paul's room and strike up another game. It didn't matter if she won or loss. She just wanted to play the game again. Or any game. With him.

Uh oh. This was bad.

Madison left the chief's office. She walked past the patient wing of the hospital. She itched to go back inside Paul's room. Not to talk about his back or her nerves. She didn't want to talk at all. She just wanted to kick her feet up on the bed and sit quietly beside him. She'd never had that feeling before. It was the opposite of non-attached. It was a feeling she couldn't afford.

Like when she was a child, Madison couldn't sit still or be quiet any longer. She had to get out of there. Running away was the only answer. And so she left the hospital to head back to her hotel room. This time, no one came after her with a scolding.

The late afternoon sun streamed into the hospital room. Paul eyed the Connect Four game board sitting on the bedside table. The black and red pieces filled the entire chute. The stalemate from last night stood.

Madison hadn't returned last night. She hadn't come in this morning during rounds. He listened hard for the clacking of her heels on the linoleum floor. But he was greeted at each turn with the squeaking protests of visitors' soled sneakers, the tapping superiority of doctor's loafers, and the quiet calm of nurses' mules.

When two sets of loafers stopped outside his door, Paul slumped down in the bed. He slumped even further when Chief Pena and Dr. Lamb came inside.

"How are you feeling today, Major Hanson?" asked the chief.

"Like I could dance the merengue."

The chief chuckled. Dr. Lamb's lips spread when the chief turned to include him in on the joke. But the moment the chief's back was turned, Lamb's fake grin turned into a real scowl.

"We hope to get you out of here soon," the chief was saying. "I believe Dr. Gray explained the parameters of the spinal fusion surgery."

"She did."

"I just want to make sure you understand all the particulars before you make a final decision."

The older man went into a litany of processes and contraindications that Madison had already gone over. Paul didn't hear much of what Chief Pena said. He was too busy looking over his shoulder for any sign of Madison. When it was clear she wasn't coming, Paul started listening out for any censure for what the chief had walked in on last night. He couldn't detect a single note of reproach there either.

"And if I don't want surgery?" said Paul after the chief paused to see if he had any questions.

That perked up Lamb. The other man inhaled loudly, reminding Paul once again that he could be a minion of Darth Vader.

"These sensations and numbness, they come and go," said Paul. "There's the possibility that one day it'll just stay gone without me going under the knife again."

"There is that possibility," said the chief. "But I don't like the odds."

"Dr. Lamb initially thought it might be a possibility," said Paul.

Lamb sniffed loudly again, a wheezing sound that was definitely like Darth Vader. "That was before we ran all the tests."

"You mean the tests Dr. Gray insisted on?" asked Paul.

"The tests we both needed to make an informed decision."

"Dr. Gray seemed to have the right answer even before the test results."

Lamb narrowed his gaze at Paul. Paul was certain that if the man had any access to the force, he'd be using it to choke Paul right now.

"The good news," said Chief Pena, "is that you have two of the best doctors on staff available to perform your surgery. You couldn't be in better hands."

The thought of going under and having Lamb operate on him did not appeal to Paul. The thought of being in Madison's care warmed him through. Just the thought of it made his toes tingle.

A pager went off. Chief Pena looked down at the device on his hip. "I'm sorry. I have to get this. Dr. Lamb, will you stay behind and answer any of Major Hanson's questions?"

The chief didn't wait for a response. He turned on his loafer'd heel. With a couple of barely audible squeaks, he was out of the door.

Paul looked up at Lamb. Lamb looked down at him. The man straightened his back in a move likely meant to show dominance. Paul didn't feel in the least cowed. If this were a fistfight, Paul would win with one hand tied behind his back and his legs still incapacitated. Lamb stepped back toward the door as though he sensed the odds.

"You should know I have extensive experience with this surgery," said Lamb. "You'll be in the best hands with me on this operation."

"Madison's doing my surgery. And that's only if I decide to go through with it."

Paul hadn't decided to go through with it yet.

He'd only told the nurse last night that he was leaning toward it. And that had only been when he thought it would bring him closer to Madison.

He knew he was a bit touched in the head to make such a monumental decision based on what was going on in his heart. But if he couldn't trust the woman he was falling for with his life, then he didn't know what the point of it all was.

"You might not go through with it?" Lamb looked as though Paul had just spoken Mandarin. Then he looked back to the door. "Wait? Is that why she's not here?"

"Who?"

"Madison." Lamb looked down at the chart as though he was speaking to it and not Paul. "If she knows you're not going through with this surgery, then she's probably off to find another. I should've known it."

Lamb balled his hands into fists. Paul was surprised that the man didn't stomp his foot like a child who was told he had to share his favorite toy.

"This has just been a waste of my time." Lamb rubbed one of his fists at his temple as he laughed to himself. "And to think I thought there was actually something between you two."

Paul knew he should lend credence to the denial

that anything was going on between him and Madison. He knew that any impropriety could cost her her job. But he couldn't make his mouth work because his heart knew there was something between them. His gaze went back to the Connect Four game. Lamb's eyes went there too.

"Did you play that game with her?" asked Lamb, his features screwing into uncertainty again. "She never loses."

"She didn't lose," said Paul. "It's a stalemate."

"Madison doesn't do stalemates," said Lamb. "She doesn't do shades of gray. She wins. And if she loses, she'll come back harder. She's not going to stop until she gets this promotion."

Paul didn't ask what promotion, which seemed to tick Lamb off more. But Paul wasn't an idiot. He'd figured from that first day when Madison and Lamb fought over his wheelchair, they were in a battle over something bigger. Paul was just thankful it was a job and not a relationship between them.

"You should know this job is just a stepping stone for her. She's a city girl. She'll leave in a few years."

Now that was something Paul worried over. He saw himself walking toward Madison. He saw himself sweeping her off her feet. He saw her swollen belly with his child. He saw them living happily ever after here on a ranch surrounded by horses and friends and their children.

He wanted to deny Lamb's prediction of how this would all end. But when he looked up, Lamb was already halfway out the door. The door closed with a quiet snick as his loafers squeaked down the hall.

CHAPTER SIXTEEN

*M*adison was tired. She was tired of the firm hotel mattress. She was tired of the continental breakfast. She was tired of the tiny soaps and shampoos.

She wanted to walk out the door to her own yard. She wanted to drown in shampoo. She wanted to sleep on memory foam that only knew her body. She wanted to be held by the tall, broad form of the man in her dreams.

Except she was awake. She was awake, but she clearly saw the form of the man she wanted her mattress to remember in her mind's eye.

She punched at her pillows. Unfortunately, that move did nothing to make her more comfortable.

Nor did it shake the vision of Paul Hanson from her head.

What would make her feel better was to get a scalpel in her hand and slip into an OR. There were other patient charts piling up on her desk. She should be focused on one of them and not one who could cost her everything she was working for.

Slipping into a pair of her mother's heels, Madison headed out to start her day. When she walked into the hospital, all seemed quiet. Which was never a good sign at a hospital.

She walked straight to her office, avoiding the patient ward. When she'd left the other day, she'd left with a clear desk. All of her files had been neatly organized and put away. Now there was a new stack on her desk. Papers spilled out from the manilla folders.

Madison gave a happy sigh. This was exactly what she needed. A stack of someone else's problems to solve. She pulled out her desk chair and prepared to dig in.

"I'm surprised to find you here."

Madison didn't look up at the sound of Doug's voice. She was not in the mood to deal with him today. But the sound of his loafers pacing against the floor grated her nerves and broke her concentration.

She did look up then, and she was confronted with a stranger. Doug looked like an irate child with his pinched expression, a child who had everything handed to him on a platter. He had a superior air to him. Most of it earned.

Doug was brilliant. She couldn't deny it. But had there been anything else that had attracted her to him?

Madison couldn't think of a single thing. All she could remember was how the two of them would compete. Had that been it? Had she just wanted a good fight?

She didn't fight with Paul, not really. And it wasn't really a competition. Not when each time she came at him, he completely disarmed her. With a grin, or a joke, or a few words that caught her totally off guard. It felt nice to be off guard and not itching for a fight.

"So, you won the surgery," said Doug.

"What surgery?"

"Don't play coy. The Hanson surgery. He as much as said so."

"He did?" Madison stood. "He said he'd do it."

Joy infused her. She wanted to twirl around.

Paul was going to do the surgery. She promptly forgot that she was trying to stay away from him and rushed to the door to get to his floor. But there was a Doug-sized obstruction blocking her way.

"This isn't over, Madison. I've racked up two other surgeries while you've been playing footsie. I'm still in the running."

In the running? Oh, he meant for the Chief of Orthopedic Surgery position. Which was what she'd come here for. But right now, she just wanted to double-check that Paul actually said he'd do the surgery.

"Good for you, Doug." Madison slipped around him and headed to the patient wing.

When she got to Paul's room, he had a packed house. His friends were all around him. It wasn't hard to find him, though. Not because he was the one on the bed. Because he was the only one whose smile didn't reach his eyes.

Paul looked tired. He looked weary. He looked a little sad.

"Paul?"

His gaze found hers. There was a spark that flared, but it didn't ignite like it had before when he looked at her.

"Can you all clear the room," Madison said to the people gathered. "I need to check on my patient."

There was a chorus of yeses and thank you docs. Madison ignored them all. Her gaze fixed on Paul, who had turned to look at the Connect Four game board, which was still in the stalemate they'd left it in the night before.

"How are you feeling?" she said.

Paul's gaze made its way back to her. There was an accusation in his eyes. She had no idea what it was for? What had she done?

"I hear I'm going on a date soon," Madison tried.

"Yeah? You and Dr. Lamb rekindling the old magic?"

"With Doug? Ew, no."

Paul quirked an eyebrow. A smile touched the corner of his mouth. But again, it didn't reach his eyes.

Madison took another step toward him. She knew she was walking a fine line, but she couldn't stop the forward motion. "There's this guy who said he'd take me on a date if I did his surgery."

"Yeah?" Paul cocked his head to the side. "I think I know that guy. You should stay away from him because he plays for keeps."

"I think he's getting the short end of the stick

because he has no idea how much I can throw down in a restaurant."

Paul snorted. When he took a clearing breath, his smile touched his eyes. "So, you're not one of those dainty salad eaters, I take it."

"I like a salad. On the side of my steak."

She was standing within touching distance of him. She could touch him. Maybe use her stethoscope to listen to his heartbeat. That's what his doctor would do. Except she wasn't wearing a stethoscope. She had not a single medical apparatus with her. She didn't even have his chart in her hands for cover.

"You scared?" she asked.

"Yeah," he said.

"I'm the best, Paul. And I promise I'm going to do my very best with you."

He took her hand and tugged her closer until she was sitting on the bed. "I believe you're the very best, Maddie. I'm not scared of the surgery. I'm scared of after the surgery."

"Fine, I'll order the chicken instead."

He chuckled, and his gaze lit up. Madison finally felt a sense of relief, a sense of rightness. But the light in his eyes flickered, and his smile dimmed.

"This will earn you that promotion?" he said. "Winning my surgery over Lamb?"

Oh, that's why Paul was upset. Probably why Doug was upset. Doug could never keep anything to himself. Not his words, not his kisses, not his promises.

"I can see by the look in your eyes that it's true," said Paul.

Madison scooted closer so that this man could see into the heart of her. "I'm going to earn that promotion because I'm the best at what I do."

"And then you'll leave. Because working here at Mercy General is just a stepping stone?"

"Who said that? Doug? That jerk." Madison rubbed at her forehead as though she could wipe Doug out of her consciousness. "This is where my dad's from. He and my mom left me their place in New York, but it never felt like home. I thought maybe this might feel like home. It feels like a place where I can make a difference."

Paul pulled her close. Madison knew she should resist. But it felt like she'd been there before. It felt like a memory. It felt like home.

"You can have the steak on our date," Paul said. "Lobster, too. I think that will cover the cost of my surgery."

He rested his forehead against hers. They were so very close to each other. If she tilted her head, she could kiss him.

Memories were often the past repeating itself. So it didn't surprise Madison that in this moment, just like it had happened before, that there was the sound of a throat clearing at the door.

CHAPTER SEVENTEEN

Paul watched as Madison shut her eyes and clenched her fingers. The pain etched there made his heart ache. It made his gut wrench. It made his toes twitch.

He ignored the sensation in his limbs and reached for her. He took her hand in his and unfurled her fingers. He reached his other hand to her brow and smoothed out the creases he found there.

Madison opened her eyes and looked at him. For one perfect moment, no one else in the world existed but the two of them. In that perfect moment, Paul saw his life flash before him.

Not the events of the past that those near death saw as they were near dying. No, Paul saw his future as it was going to be because he was going to live. He was going to live the rest of his days with this woman.

He saw her kicking those heels off after a long day of surgery and running to him. He'd catch her in his arms and twirl her around in a field of green. A stable of horses would whinny their approval as their trainer sipped from the lips of the woman he adored, the woman he loved.

He loved her.

The hard facts of that singular truth knocked the breath out of him. He'd always known that when he fell in love, it would be hard. The landing into this reality smarted but in the best way possible.

A chuckle escaped his lips. Madison's lips parted as she gazed up at him. He'd been so near to kissing her just a second ago before they were interrupted.

In Paul's mind, a scene from the end of *The Return of the Jedi* played in bright technicolor. It was the scene where Leia and Han were trapped on Tatooine. There were stormtroopers at Han's back, and it looked like all was lost. Until Leia revealed that she had a blaster.

"I love you," Paul said, just as the anti-hero of the film had said to the princess when danger was at their backs.

Madison didn't repeat Leia's line. But she had to know. Even though they'd been caught, he had to make his feelings known.

Instead of a blaster to take down the intruders in the doorway, Paul pulled Madison to her and stole a kiss. She might as well have had a blaster because the moment his lips impacted hers, everything inside him was blown apart.

Paul's heart raced when Madison pressed into him. Her pulse raced at the base of her neck, where he held her. It matched the quickened pace of his own heart. If he hadn't already been laying prone, his knees would've gone weak.

"Dr. Gray, may I see you?"

Breaking apart from Madison was the hardest thing Paul ever had to do in his life. And he'd seen three tours and come far too close to an explosive. But nothing matched the tingling jolt of Madison's kiss. He felt empty and void when she pulled away from him.

Madison's eyes didn't leave Paul as she stood. She swallowed as she set her features, removing all traces of the desire she'd shown him only a second ago. She began to turn away from him, beyond his grasp. Then she took a step, and he could not follow.

"Maddie," he called after her.

She paused. But she did not turn. Her shoulders went back as though she was preparing to face a firing squad. It wasn't stormtroopers with blasters. It wasn't Dr. Vader in his white coat.

Chief Pena raised a brow as he looked at Paul. Paul supposed that was too familiar a name to call his surgeon. But then again, kissing his surgeon was likely far worse an offense.

"I know what this looks like," Paul said to the elderly doctor.

"I don't think you do, Major."

"It looks like Dr. Gray was fraternizing with a patient. But I'm not just any patient. I'm going to marry her one day."

Madison's shoulders straightened. "He's joking."

"No," said Paul. "I'm definitely not joking. But I'm not going to ask her to marry me until after the surgery, so there won't be any hypocrisy."

Madison huffed a breath as she whirled back around. "It's Hippocratic, not hypocrisy. And that's not what's happening here."

Paul looked past Madison to the man in the doorway. Chief Pena didn't look angry as he regarded the two of them. He looked pensive, as though the two of them were a complicated puzzle that he was deciding where to begin his problem-solving.

"You're a fine man, Major Hanson," said Chief Pena. "Dr. Gray could certainly do a lot worse."

"Thank you," said Paul. His chest puffed up under the compliment. But when he looked to Madison, she looked crestfallen.

"She might one day become your wife," said Chief Pena. "But, unfortunately, she can never be your surgeon."

The tingles that had started in Paul's toes crept higher. He felt them in his shins, and the back of his knees, and now higher up his thighs. He wondered if he did have the strength to stand. He needed to do something to prop Madison up. Her shoulders slumped, and her chest caved in.

"Maddie?" Paul called to her.

"Dr. Gray?" Chief Pena called to her.

Madison didn't turn to look at Paul again. She walked forward toward Chief Pena and then on past him. Paul could only lay there and watch as Madison walked out the door and followed the chief down the hall.

"What were you thinking, Madison?"

Madison had been looking out the window. She'd spent most of her life in the city, where artificial lights bloomed from every corner. It had been near impossible to see the stars. But here, in the middle of the country, where towers didn't rival the skyline, she could see every single star.

Her father had brought her out to Montana a couple of times. Normally it had been on a training exercise. He'd plant her in a hotel or on the base. Madison spent her days watching the wildlife roam free. She would lay on her back at night and look up and lose count of the stars.

Those bright orbs twinkled at her now. They

tried to coax a smile out of her. They almost caught one. Until Doug interrupted her thoughts.

"You could lose everything. And for what? Him?"

Madison turned away from the window to face off against Doug. They were inside Chief Pena's office. The chief sat behind his desk, his fingers steepled, not looking at either of them. Doug stood near the door with his hands clenched, his cheeks red.

Madison was standing, as well. She doubted she'd be in the room long enough to get comfortable in the chair. Chief Pena's silence unsettled her, making her want to pace.

She took a step away from the chief's desk and toward Doug. She didn't teeter in her heels. She stood tall. She stood a half of an inch over him. But somehow she felt even taller.

"My love life is none of your business," she said.

"Love?"

The word was a gust of wind between them both. Madison realized she'd never once considered marrying this man. Had they ever exchanged the L-word between them. It had never occurred to her to love Doug. She wondered if she ever could have?

It didn't matter anymore. Her heart was thudding more over Paul's surgery. That was the only thing that mattered; Paul needed to have that surgery.

Madison turned away from Doug and back to the chief. "You can't take me off this case."

Chief Pena didn't look angry. He didn't even look irritated or censorious. He looked thoughtful.

"I'm the best orthopedic surgeon you've got."

"Excuse me!" interjected Doug.

"All three of us know it," Madison continued, ignoring her ex.

Chief Pena placed his hands flat on his desk. His chin raised, and he nodded at her pronouncement. Madison felt a wellspring of relief.

"Are you telling me there's nothing between you and Major Hanson?" Chief Pena asked.

That wellspring of relief dried up in an instant. Madison opened her mouth to try and deny her feelings for Paul. A tidal wave of warmth rushed in to fill the spaces left behind.

"It's just harmless flirting," she tried.

"I haven't kissed any of my patients this week," said Chief Pena.

Doug exploded off the wall he'd been leaning against. "You kissed him?"

Madison ignored Doug. She was trying not to remember that kiss she'd shared with Paul. Her lips still tingled from that impact. She couldn't deny that's why she was fighting so hard to stay on this case. She needed to ensure the care of every single one of Paul's nerves. A man who could make her hair follicles tingle with just a brush of his lips needed special care.

"Would you have me believe you have no feelings for him, Madison?" asked Chief Pena. "Nothing outside of the normal care for a patient?"

Madison had to swallow a few times to tamp down the feelings that wanted to burst out of her. "I… he…"

With each word she spoke, she had to swallow again. She had to swallow hard because of the emotions bubbling inside her chest. Madison knew she had to quiet it down so that she could speak. It wasn't just Paul's life on the line here. It was her life, too.

She looked at the scalpel in a case on Pena's desk. Her hands itched to reach for it. She could remember the feel of the first scalpel she'd held. She'd picked up the instrument and felt a certainty. Her fingers never twitched when she held a scalpel because she was sure.

She remembered her hand inside Paul's. He'd given her fingers a squeeze. She'd felt the overwhelming urge to lace their hands together. It was the first time she'd felt so certain outside of an OR.

Madison looked up at the chief. He smiled knowingly at her. She sighed in defeat. Then she turned to Doug.

"Doug, if you ever cared anything for me, I need you now."

CHAPTER NINETEEN

Paul was tired. He was tired of lying down. He was tired of waiting around.

He felt no tingling in his toes. No hot and cold sensations in his legs. All the sensation was in his heart. His heart beat so fiercely, so rapidly that Paul was certain it was going to burst out of his chest. Maybe that would make Madison come back sooner.

With a glance up at the door, he saw that that wasn't happening. Paul was done waiting. He hefted his left leg up. With a grunt, he slid it off the edge of the hospital bed. It took an effort to keep his balance, but he managed. Finally, he was able to swing his right leg over the side of the bed.

He looked down to confirm that his toes were touching the cold ground. They were. But he felt nothing.

He felt nothing in his feet. Nothing in his legs. Nothing in his chest… except an ache.

Madison hadn't come back to his room last night. He hadn't seen her at all this morning. He had no clue what her fate had been with her boss.

Was she kicked off his case? Was she still employed at the hospital? What if they'd forced her to leave town altogether? He had to find her.

He began a rocking motion. Pressing his fists into the uncomfortable hospital mattress, he gave a heave, but not the ho. He looked down again to make sure his feet had contact with the floor.

They did. Not that he could feel the cold of the linoleum. It was no matter. He was going to stand. He was going to find the woman he wanted to sweep into his arms. If she wasn't welcome here any longer, then he wasn't staying either.

Taking in a deep breath, Paul leaned back, readying himself to both heave and ho, when the door to his room creaked open. Paul's head jerked up, readying to launch himself at Madison. Unfortunately, coming into the room was the last person in the world Paul wanted to have in his arms, or even in his vicinity.

"What are you doing?" demanded Dr. Lamb.

"About to go for my morning run," said Paul. "What does it look like?"

"Do not get up."

Lamb held out his hand like a stop sign. As if that would've stopped Paul.

"If you fall down and get a concussion, she'll blame me."

"She?" Paul looked over Dr. Lamb's shoulder. But he didn't see her. "Where is she?"

"She's not here. It's part of the deal."

"Part of what deal?"

"The deal she made to get me to perform your surgery."

"I don't want you to perform my surgery. I want her to do it."

"That's against the rules. Doctors can't operate on loved ones."

Dr. Lamb crinkled his nose as he spat out those last two words. Paul didn't care that he'd mangled them. The words were music to his ears.

"Loved ones?" Paul asked.

Lamb fixed his features, but irritation and disbelief shadowed his eyes. "It's just an expression."

"She said she loved me?"

"It's just an expression," Lamb insisted. "It's a good policy because, clearly, her personal feelings are impairing her professional judgment."

"Madison said she has personal feelings for me?"

Lamb let out a sigh of defeat. "I don't know what she sees in you. You don't seem very bright. For example, it's not wise to antagonize the man who is about to cut into your back with a sharp knife."

"Oh, I'm not worried about you."

"You should be." Lamb tried for menace, but he looked like a disgruntled Ewok with his mane of blond curls.

"Well, I'm not. You're too focused on winning the game."

"She was focused on the same thing at one point."

"She still is. You're just playing different games now. You're playing at that doctor game—what's it called? The one where you buzz the sides if you don't have a steady hand."

"It's called Operation, and I never buzzed the sides in that game."

"Madison's not playing that. She's playing the Game of Life. And she's swept the whole board."

"Yeah?" said Dr. Lamb. "Well, you just better

hope I don't buzz the edges of your insides with my scalpel."

"You won't. Like you said, if I get hurt, she'll kill you. And I have every confidence she could take you."

Lamb nodded as though Paul was right.

CHAPTER TWENTY

Madison paced the length of the hall. Her heels clacked against the linoleum. The sound of boots accompanied her pacing.

Luke walked in the opposite direction of her. She and Paul's best friend would meet in the middle, about-face, and head in the other direction. When they met the wall, they'd turn and repeat the process.

"The two of you are driving me crazy," said Elaine. "He's going to be fine."

"I've never been on this side of the OR," said Madison. "I'm always the one holding the scalpel."

Luke held her hand. Elaine grabbed the other. They paced together as a unit. It was the first time

Madison had walked with others beside her. It was the first time she'd been in a waiting room. When her father had passed, she hadn't even been in the same state. She'd been all by herself, as no family remained. Not even Aunt Bess. Just like when she'd taken that walk home, she'd been all alone.

She wasn't by herself now. Luke and Elaine weren't the only two people in the waiting room. The room was filled to the brim with people from the Purple Heart Ranch. Soldiers, wives, children, and others who worked there.

Madison had met Paul's new employer. A female cattle rancher who stood tall in stylish boots. Brenda Vance waited patiently for news from the surgery, just as she was waiting patiently for her new horse wrangler to make it to his first day of work. Brenda didn't doubt that Paul would recover and be on the job soon. She must get that certainty from her pastor brother, who kept nodding calmly at Madison as though he was receiving word from up high that all would be well soon.

Paul had so many people who cared about him. Each person had come up and embraced Madison as though she was someone special, someone important.

How had this happened?

She'd only arrived here a few days ago. Only knew Paul for such a short amount of time. And, now, it felt like she was ensconced into the center of his world. It was a place she never wanted to leave.

It was a place that felt like a memory.

It was a place she wanted to call home.

It didn't matter to her if Paul ever stood again. Madison wanted to rest her head against this chest. She wanted to curl into his embrace. She wanted him to kiss her again. And then again, and then some more for the rest of her days.

The doors to the OR opened. A single doctor came out. His expensive loafers made no sound against the shiny floor as he walked toward them.

Madison held still. She knew every look on Doug's face. Right now, he had on a poker face that she'd never seen.

"He's resting," said Doug. "I believe the operation was a success."

There was a sigh of relief from everyone. But not Madison. She demanded to see Paul's charts, wanting to check Doug's every step and stitch.

"Dr. Gray, you can check my charts later. Right now, he wants to see you."

Madison dashed around Doug. But then she

stopped. She turned and gave him a hug. "Thank you."

Doug didn't squeeze her back. He patted her awkwardly, in the way a surgeon not used to the gratitude of his patient's family.

When Madison came into the room, Paul was resting with his eyes closed. She walked quietly, slowly, toward him. Her heart rate jumped with every step. It felt like she was being shocked with paddles with each beat.

The rules had prevented her from operating on a loved one. She'd followed the rules. Because Paul was a loved one. Madison was desperately in love with this man.

His eyes opened. "Hey," he said with a lazy grin. "Either I survived. Or this is heaven. Doesn't matter which as long as you're here."

"We're still here on earth."

Madison took his hand. Her fingers curled around his until they were laced together. That certainty she always felt when she'd held a scalpel came over her when his long fingers pressed against hers.

Madison knew she would be a surgeon for the rest of her life. Maybe not chief of Orthopedic Surgery immediately. But someday. She knew that as certainly as she knew she would be with this man for the rest of her life. Not someday. Right now.

"You owe me a date," said Paul.

"Already taken care of. Dinner will be served later tonight when you're ready to eat."

"You bought me dinner?"

"No, I didn't buy it. It's on your hospital bill."

Paul chuckled, and it was the most beautiful sound she'd ever heard. But the laughter died from his throat, and he sobered. "Did you lose the promotion?"

Madison shrugged. "For now. But Doug won't stay long. He's a city boy."

"Aren't you a city girl?"

"My roots are country strong."

"With those heels?"

"Hey!"

His grin spread wider. His hand lifted to her cheek. There was still a blood pressure cuff attached to his right arm. The nubs of ECG leads were visible beneath his thin hospital gown. Madison heard the beeping of the monitors speed up. The sounds kept pace with her own racing pulse and heartbeat.

"So, you're going to stick around?" Paul asked. "You're not going back to the city?"

"Maybe for a day trip to get a nice pair of

designer cowboy boots," she said as she leaned into his hand. "Otherwise, I'm good right where I am."

"Maddie?"

"Hmmm?" She nuzzled into the center of his palm.

"Since you're not my doctor anymore, it's not against the rules for me to steal a kiss."

Her eyes blinked open, and she gazed at this man who had stolen her heart while she'd been trying to read his medical chart. "Can't steal what someone gives to you."

Madison leaned into Paul. She pressed him back to the pillows when he tried to meet her halfway. When her lips met his, she was kissing a wide grin. It tasted delicious. It tasted of hope, of happiness, of love.

"That was amazing," Paul said with a sigh. "It made my toes tingle."

They both glanced down at the bottom of the bed. The sheet moved as his wriggled the toes of both his feet. It was a great sign, it meant he would stand. For now, Madison allowed him to sweep her into his arms as she deepened the kiss.

Want to learn more about the place where Paul is going to work?
Meet his boss Brenda Vance when she falls for an Army Ranger in
"The Rancher takes his Convenient Bride,"
Book One in the Rangers of Purple Heart Ranch!

And stay tuned for more stories straight from the heart of the Purple Heart Ranch.

THE RANCHER TAKES HIS CONVENIENT BRIDE EXCERPT

Keaton could hear his heart pounding in his ears. Just like every time he was on the battlefield, the beats synced with the ticking of the second hand of a clock. A calm went over him in the face of the danger that awaited him. He inhaled, the oxygen adding fuel to the bravado that came naturally to him. He was a well-trained soldier, a superbly trained warrior. One of the best specimens of the 75th Ranger Regiment.

Stepping out of his hidey-hole where he'd taken cover after the first shots rang out, Keaton looked around. His sightline was clear, which did not bode well. His spidey senses tingled at the calm and quiet. War was a noisy, frenetic affair.

Something was wrong.

Keeping low to the ground, he poked his head out to gather more intel. The camouflage of his clothes made it so that he blended with his environment. Even his gun was painted green and brown to mix in with the elements.

And then he heard it. A cry. A shot.

They sounded one after the other. Keaton's ears perked like a dog coming alert. Before storming into action, he deduced what he'd learned.

The cry had come from the left side. The shot had come from behind him. The blast from the gun had gone over his head. The cry from a human throat had come before the shot. There was no resulting thump of a body.

A tingle went up to his spine. Keaton rolled over onto his back just in time. A grizzly bear of a man was on him, weapon rising.

That's where the bear went wrong. A rising weapon was completely ineffective. Keaton's weapon was at the ready. His finger already on the trigger, which he squeezed.

The grizzly's body jerked from the direct hit. Pink paint-splattered exactly where his heart would lay if the traitor had one. Keaton fired off another and then another round.

"Hey," growled the grizzly man. "I'm down."

"You know you're on my team, right?" said Keaton.

Griffin "Grizz" Hayes grinned. His incisors glinted in the midday sun like a predator who knew he'd cornered his prey. Keaton knew that look. It was the same look Grizz had given him back in Basic Training when he decided to prank their drill sergeant.

Sergeant Cook never saw it coming. The sadistic sergeant never figured out who'd put Gorilla Glue on the inside of his hat. The entire squad had paid for that prank for months in extra drills in the middle of the night. But it had been worth it to stick it to that demon-born drill sergeant. The red marks of the glue had taken just as long to heal, reminding the soldiers of their revenge every day they ate mud and missed sleep.

So, why had Grizz turned on his best friend now? And why was he grinning after he'd been caught? The spidey tingles crawled over Keaton's skin again.

Keaton didn't remain glued to his spot. He hit the ground just as more shots rang out. Grizz let out a roar of laughter. So, it was a mutiny. His entire team was out to get him.

What for?

It couldn't be the late-night planning session Keaton held them in until well after one in the morning last Saturday. It couldn't be the fact that Keaton changed his mind twice, on which supplier to use, causing them to redo the books over again, and then again. It couldn't be the fact that he'd promised General Strauss that his team would have their Ranger Training Camp ready in just ninety days when the team had originally planned to take half a year to get things in gear, which didn't include any downtime after separating from the military.

The shots coming at him from all four directions told Keaton he was wrong. They'd divided into two equal teams, three on each. But the four remaining men all aimed their weapons at him.

Keaton was undaunted. As the leader of his team, he saw how he could use this mutiny as a teachable moment. A plan formed in his mind. He only had time to come up with two variables in case Plan A didn't work instead of his standard three. With the main plan and two backups, he moved into action.

Mac Kenzie's gaze connected with his. The recognition dawned in Mac's eyes. The two had been in many tough situations together. Enough that they could communicate without using words.

So Mac, or Mackenzie as everyone simply

pushed his first and last name together, saw Keaton's entire plan in one glance. But again, Keaton was already locked and loaded a second before Mac rose to the occasion.

Keaton grabbed Mac by the shoulders. Rolling him over, Keaton sprang onto his feet, hefting all of Mac's six foot three, two-hundred-fifty-pound bulk of pure muscle.

"You son of a—" But Mac's words died as his body jerked, taking on pink and purple paint from the assault meant for Keaton.

Keaton swung his weapon up and under Mac's armpit. He took aim and fired, towing Jordan Spinelli and David Porco.

With two down, he had two more to go. He ducked around Grizz, plastering his front to the man's paint-smeared back. In a matter of seconds, Grizz's front matched his back. But not a speck got on Keaton.

From the protection of Grizz's massive bulk, Keaton opened fire on his last frenemy. Russell "Rusty" Hook, who was a perfect shot, went down immediately.

Keaton still didn't lower his weapon. "Surrender," he called out.

"Never," the five men said in unison. "Surrender

is not a Ranger word." They all chuckled after reciting the end of the Ranger Creed.

Keaton lowered his weapon. He walked to Mac and helped the man up. Another part of the creed was that they never left a fallen comrade under any circumstances.

Keaton clapped Spinelli on his back and came away with pink and purple paint.

"Told you he had eyes in the back of his head," said Porco.

"Don't be ridiculous," said Keaton. "I have 360 vision. Like a hawk."

"You mean an owl," said Grizz. The man was the strong, silent type women always swooned over. He could often be found reading ancient poetry books. But the weird part was that Grizz actually liked the riddle of words.

"Then I'm a super owl," Keaton countered. "Anyway, I think we can all learn something from this."

Five groans joined the chorus of chirping crickets and birdsong in the forest. Keaton thought he heard a paint gun safety click off.

"This was supposed to be a fun excursion in the midst of your insane work plan," said Mac.

"Don't knock the plan," said Keaton. "The plan is our ticket to not go to desk jobs."

After separating from service, many rangers went on to work in the intelligence community or in top-level security. But none of his guys wanted to work inside. They all craved the outdoors and the freedom to set their own schedules. There was still a lot of action in them. They just no longer had the desire to travel and dodge real bullets.

"The unexpected will happen to us as we move forward building the best training camp in these United States," said Keaton. "But, we'll always be ready to maneuver because we have a plan."

"Oh yeah?" said Rusty. "Maneuver this."

Keaton dodged the paint pellet. It caught him in the forearm, but it wasn't a direct hit.

Rusty rolled his eyes.

"Like a hawk," Keaton grinned.

"An owl," corrected Grizz.

Keaton shrugged.

"You sure about this location, though?" said Grizz. "The Purple Heart Ranch in Montana?"

"I've heard some crazy things happening up there," said Spinelli.

Keaton had heard them too. Soldiers going to heal the wounds they'd received in combat. Yet, in less than three months, each man had winded up in holy matrimony and no plans to leave the ranch. It was kind of like a cult. But Keaton knew the man in charge and knew him to be a top-notch soldier and a decent man.

Marriage wasn't a path Keaton planned to go down. He had a five-year plan before he even thought about marriage.

"We're not living on the land, so none of the rules or hoodoo will apply to us," he assured his men. "Our clients will stay six weeks, at the longest, which doesn't meet their three-month rule."

Apparently, the land of the Purple Heart Ranch had a zoning issue where if a soldier wanted to live on it, they had to be married within three months or hightail it out of there. It was backwoods, for sure. But they needed land in the backwoods to create their state-of-the-art course and facility.

"Good," said Grizz. "Cause myth or zoning, I have no plans for a wife."

There was a chorus of agreement. Except for Mac and Rusty. Mac had given a woman a ring, which she'd rejected more than once. Rusty had divorce papers sitting in his duffel bag. There was one signature on the ream of paperwork. It wasn't his signature.

"Let's get changed and head out," said Keaton. "We've got a lot of work to do and little time to do it.

Living at the edge of a rehabilitation ranch and preparing for our first clients will keep us all too busy for dating."

"Whoa, whoa," said Porco, holding his hands up in surrender. "Put dating back in the plan. Those farm girls need a load of me in their lives."

Pops rang out as Porco was painted with a shower of bullets for that comment. With their ire turned away from himself, Keaton took a rare moment to relax and laugh at his brothers-in-arms and their antics.

His edict stood. With the amount of work they had to do in the next three months, none of them, himself especially, had time for dating. The training facility would be his sweetheart for the next five years before he even decided to look for a wife. That was the plan.

CHAPTER TWO

The sizzle of charred beef smelled different when said cow was alive and kicking and not quartered into pieces and placed in a pan. Brenda Vance backed up. She avoided the bull's hindquarters, but she wasn't quick enough to avoid the wood. The plank of the fencing splintered, and a shard of wood caught the side of her forehead.

Blood mixed with sweat and caught in her eye. Brenda swore. Her muttered curse made the younger three of her ranch hands wince. They should all wince. It was their fault the cow wasn't properly secure.

"You all right, missy?" came the gravely, tobacco tarnished voice of the fourth and eldest ranch hand. Manuel Bautista had stepped on this ranch around the time when Brenda had taken her first steps before she'd turned a year old. Like her, he knew this place inside and out. Unlike her, he was not the one in charge.

Brenda bit her tongue before she could utter another curse. Her brother might be a pastor, but she'd learned that his role didn't give her any extra free passes for the next life.

"Don't call me missy." She swiped the blood and sweat with her worn flannel shirt, getting a whiff of the hard work she put in this day. Looking up, she saw that two of the ranch hands' hands barely glistened in the hot afternoon sun. Their brand-new cowboy hats were starched perfect. Their shirts had not a single drop of sweat at the pits.

"It's Miss Vance," she said as she stared down at the blood on her shirt. "Or, boss."

As the elder ranch hand turned back to calm the new bull, Brenda caught the sound of a Spanish curse. Two of the other men chuckled. The skinny blond one in tight jeans that most certainly came from either Old Navy or Urban Outfitters was the one Brenda had nicknamed Yankee. The second chuckler, the one Brenda called Frat Boy, had a T-shirt with Greek letters stretched over his brown biceps. He'd claimed his great grandfather was one of the famed Buffalo soldiers. Though Brenda doubted that this kid came from that strong stock when he constantly swatted and yelped when any bug came near him, or any mark landed on any piece of his wardrobe.

The other hand didn't laugh. He pretended to look away. Not to be above it all. His attempt to not take a side was clear. His name Brenda knew. He was Angel Bautista, the nephew of her ornery elder ranch hand.

Angel was young, just out of high school. Born in a time where girls were told they could do or be anything, and they had examples and paths to follow. Angel's uncle had been born during a time when women's places were in the kitchen. Or, if she wanted to venture outside, in the garden.

The other two hands were outsiders. This was a semester internship for them. They'd be back to their city colleges in a couple of weeks' time. Whereas Angel lived here and would need to find and keep work on a ranch. He was stuck between two worlds with two elders to mind. Brenda wouldn't wait long to figure out who the kid would follow.

This was her life, her livelihood, and she needed good hands to keep it going. She'd been herding cattle just as long as she been riding horses. She'd been bruised feeding livestock. Broken a toe while changing out a horseshoe. A broken wrist while on a cattle run which she'd led on her own. You name it, she sprained it, strained, and might even have fractured it at some point in her line of work as the overseer on this ranch. And through it all, she'd never missed a day of work.

Brenda had done it on her own the last three years after her parents retired. But in those many years, she'd made the ranch so profitable that she'd grown the herd, thereby increasing the workload and the need for hands to help her.

With these sorry excuses for hands, she might as well be doing it on her own. Manuel refused to listen to her way of doing things, relying instead on the old ways. And the other men followed behind him, even though she was the one who signed their paychecks.

"Maybe you should head back inside the house," said Manuel. "To tend to your injury. It's dangerous work out here."

He left off the end of his sentence *for a woman*. At least he learned one lesson today.

This had all stemmed from her suggestion that they use sugar as well as grain to corral the new bull she'd just purchased so that they could brand it. Sugar would've helped calm the animal down. But it was a new way of doing things, and Manuel had balked. Then the bull had kicked out.

Brenda was too tired to fight. The blood still dripping in her eyes was making it hard to oversee what they were doing. She knew they weren't doing it the way she wanted them to do it. But the bull was branded, signifying that she was the owner. That was the major item on her to-do list for the day, so she might as well call it a day.

She banged through the back door of the big house and froze. The back door led directly into the house's kitchen. Dinner was sizzling in a pan. A perfectly cooked steak alongside roasted smashed potatoes just out of the oven and buttered green beans. The fridge was opened and a body hunched down inside. The door closed, and a man in an apron stood.

"You are truly a gift from God," said Brenda.

"And you're bleeding from the crown of your head," said the man. "But I don't see any thorns."

Brenda touched her hand to her forehead. The warm trickle of blood stained her fingertips. Luckily, there was no pain.

"If I go out there, am I going to find one of the ranch hands dead, Bren?"

Brenda sighed, disappointment clear on the gust of breath. "No, Walter. You won't be giving any last rites tonight."

Brenda's brother, Pastor Walter Vance, grabbed paper towels and pressed them to his sister's forehead.

"Ouch," she complained.

Walter ignored her. This wasn't the first time he'd cleaned her up after she'd broken skin. It had been a regular occurrence in the Vance household when they were kids. Might be one of the reasons he'd gone into the church. "Tell me what happened?"

"Incompetence. Chauvinism. Lazy ranch hands. That's what."

"I thought Bautista was one of the best?" said Walter.

"Maybe twenty years ago. The times have changed."

"Good thing that they have," said Walter. "With all the technology you've implemented into the ranch, you need fewer hands than when we were kids."

Their dad had left the ranch to both of them. But Walter gave up his share to Brenda and turned to the church. She was grateful. Especially since because her brother was not a partner, she didn't have to share with him just how much said new technology cost her, not to mention the new bull. She'd financed it, and the first payment was coming due. She didn't have enough cash liquid to keep up with all the bills and overhead.

"Bren, if something is wrong," her brother said, "you'd tell me?"

No, she wouldn't. "Of course, I would."

Brenda learned long ago that lying to a pastor didn't cause an immediate lightning strike. So, she had time. "As long as you keep coming over and cooking for me, all will be right with the world."

"Maybe you should marry," said Walter.

Brenda's utensils clattered down on the plate. This was one topic where her brother was not evolved. Brenda had no desire to get married. Men slowed her down. Case in point, her ranch hands were slowing her operation.

"You got a ranch full of soldiers next door," said Walter. "Some looking to marry in the next ninety days, as goes the regulations on the ranch land."

Which was why Brenda steered clear of her neighbors at the Purple Heart Ranch. And that included their boundary line, which forced individuals to get married just to stay on the healing ranch. She was sure the arrangement was illegal, yet no one had reported it.

"Didn't one of those soldiers run off with your fiancé?" she said.

Beth Cartwright, the pastor's daughter, had been engaged to Walter briefly. But then her childhood crush who had been MIA returned, sweeping her off her feet with a proposal and an engagement ring.

"Reese is a good man," said Walter. There was genuineness in his voice despite the bitterness of the breakup. "All of the soldiers are."

Walter was far too forgiving. But it was part of his job description. Brenda's job description was rancher. She didn't have time to be someone's wife. She was far too busy with cattle, more repair projects than she could fit on an 8 x 10 sheet of paper – single-spaced, and good for nothing ranch hands who she could see were headed to their trucks before sundown without getting their work done.

No. She was best left to her own devices. She doubted she would ever allow a man to take her hand.

CHAPTER THREE

eaton looked at the passing scenery of the American heartland. The brown, majestic mountains with peeks of various colors. The rolling green pastures that seemed to stretch on into eternity. It surprised him how much this beautiful land mirrored the landscapes of Afghanistan, Iraq, and Syria. The only difference between the two landscapes was that hope and opportunity were in this fresh mountain air. War zones were rife with conflict, turmoil, and hopelessness.

During his service in each of those countries, Keaton had seen men die young. He'd witnessed as women and children suffered on a daily basis. He'd watched as the land was ravaged and torn apart by politics and projectiles.

Driving through the Main Street of this small Montana town, the outlook was night and day. Looking out of the window of his rented red Jeep, Keaton saw children skipping down the streets. Moms trailed behind their youth in yoga pants paired with cowboy boots. A group of old men sat on neighboring porches smoking pipes and spitting tobacco. The earthy smell of baked bread permeated the air instead of the metallic aftertaste of explosive powders.

Keaton could see why the soldiers of the Purple Heart Ranch came here and chose to stay after their rehab. The landscape held the familiarity of where they'd been. But the people showcased the future of what they were all fighting for, a community where they belonged.

For the last six years, Keaton had returned to his hometown after each assignment. The hustle and bustle of the crowded city made him anxious. The tall gray buildings and cold concrete unsettled him. The blank stares of the people on the streets, their tight lips, even the eye rolls of strangers avoiding each other on the sidewalks, made Keaton prickle with worry.

Soldiers looked at each other in the eyes. They spoke plainly. They spoke clearly.

So, no, Keaton had not mixed well with civilian life. Neither had the other men when they'd each gone back home to their city lives. None of them wanted to actively engage in combat any longer. But they still wanted a piece of the action. In this place that looked like a war zone engulfed in peace, Keaton knew that each of them might be able to make a life.

Thirty minutes later, he pulled up to the gates of the Bellflower ranch. He knew he was in the right place when he saw the purple flower insignia on the iron bars. That lily-like flower was the symbol for wounded warriors. In patches of grass just off to the side of the paved path, Keaton saw more of the purple bellflowers. They were a native plant to this area. It looked as though they grew wild on this land. No wonder the wounded vets of this ranch felt at home here.

Driving through the gates and up the gravel path, Keaton saw the ranch was filled with soldiers in various states of healing. Men with prosthetic legs rode hard on horses. Weaving farther down the bend in the road, Keaton saw a garden where men with missing fingers and missing arms tilled the soil.

Coming out of a barn were men with burns on their faces, arms, and legs. The soldiers tended to a menagerie of farm animals. Sheep and goats rubbed up against their scarred limbs as though unaware of any injury.

Keaton and his crew were fortunate that they'd return with all their limbs and faculties intact. Had any of them sustained any serious injuries, he knew this would be the best place for any soldier to come and heal. Furthermore, he hoped that any new soldiers aiming to improve their skills would come to the far side of the ranch, where he planned to build his elite training camp.

Keaton parked the Jeep at the big house where the road dead-ended. There were no numbers on any of the homes. The directions he'd been given told him to follow the road until it ended. Hopping out of the Jeep, Keaton saw the man he'd come here to meet.

Dylan Banks emerged from the double doors and marched forward. He was dressed in a denim shirt and khakis. One of his legs was tanned. The other was made of steel.

"Keaton, you made it."

"Good to see you again, Banks."

The two men clasped hands. Scarred palm met

scarred palm. Rough fingers gripped and tugged inward. The old friends came in for a hug with many claps on the back. Keaton had served with Sgt. Dylan Banks on more than one mission. The man was sharp and could improvise in difficult situations with the best of them.

"Amazing set up you have here," said Keaton. "I've heard nothing but good things about this ranch."

"We take them all," said Banks. "The tired, the poor, the huddled masses."

"Isn't that the saying on the Statue of Liberty?" Keaton chuckled.

"Well, now we're taking in the wretched refuse like Army Rangers."

Banks struck out an arm, aiming a fist at Keaton. Keaton saw the move coming and held still to receive it. It was all in good fun.

"Ah, is Banksy-wanksy still upset that he couldn't pass the Ranger PFT?"

"Shut it," said Banks, but there was no bite to his bark. "I only missed it by a couple of points. It was the water survival section that drowned me."

"You're from an island."

"I'm from New York City."

Keaton shrugged. The qualifications to become one of the elite Army Rangers were not a joke or a drill. Every month over four hundred eager souls arrived at Fort Benning, Georgia with the hopes that they might have the right stuff to accomplish the challenge. Fifty-one percent went home with their hopes dashed in the mud. The only reason Keaton had survived the training was that he'd prepared for the physical tests like a maniac.

That was what he planned to do with the training camp; train others the way he'd trained to pass the test. Boots On the Ground Elite Training was a dream Keaton didn't realize he had until he faced the nightmare that was the United States Army Ranger school. He knew he could never prepare any soldier fully for that experience. But anyone who passed through his training regimen had a better shot to be in the better half of that percentile.

"By next year, you'll be up and running," said Banks.

"Next year?" Keaton scoffed. "The plan is to open the doors in ninety days."

Banks scratched at the stubble of his jaw as he regarded Keaton. The incredulous look in his eyes said it all.

"It's ambitious," said Keaton. "I know. But I have

a well thought out plan that will work if executed properly."

"Of course, you do," Banks chuckled, clapping Keaton on the back again. "I believe you can do it. Amazing things can happen in ninety days, especially on this ranch."

Now it was Keaton's turn to scratch at the stubble on his chin. He knew what that reference meant. Many of the men who came here to heal wound up getting married in that time period. Rumor had it, it wasn't just the zoning laws that governed occupancy on the ranch. Many believed it was something about the land itself.

Keaton was not a superstitious man. Even with that, he had no plans to live on the land. He only needed to work on it. So, the rules and the myths would have no bearing on him nor his business.

"Let's go take a look at the parcel your leasing," said Banks.

They hopped into a golf cart and took off. If Keaton thought the land was beautiful from afar, it was breathtaking up close. Colors kept switching from green pastures, to fertile brown dirt, to a rainbow riot of blooms. Interspersed were horses of brown, white, and black. Sheep with fluffy poofs of hair … and an array of the rangiest mutts he'd ever seen.

Five dogs barked as they drove by. A few of them had a prosthetic attachment. One even had a wheelchair attached to his hind legs.

"Those are mine," said Dylan. "Well, they're my wife's. But they came with her in the marriage, so …"

Keaton didn't bother to question the strangeness of this place any further. He kept his gaze trained on the land, making mental notes of how his clients would access the training facilities. At the edge of the ranch, Keaton saw his vision come to life. There, in the untouched land, was where he would carve out a dry patch from a mud pit where his students would learn the joy of crab walking, push-ups, and sit-ups.

Instead of buying lumber, they could chop down a couple of those trees to the right and make a climbing wall. The main thing they had to build was the indoor training facility and bunks. That and the specialty training area, which would take advantage of the mix of terrains from dry earth, to green pasture, to rocky hills, and the creek. That's where they'd put in installations to train special forces for covert missions.

"Can you pull up closer to the creek?" asked Keaton.

Instead of pulling closer, Banks slowed the vehicle. "The creek isn't within our boundaries."

It took Keaton a moment before the words made sense. When they did, his heart sank. He needed that creek for the special forces area. Heck, he needed it as part of the Ranger PFT training. Banks surely had to know that.

"It's owned by the neighboring ranch," said Banks.

"Do you think he'd be willing to sell or lease it for our purposes?" Keaton asked.

Dylan pursed his lips. "Not sure if *she* would. But you can go over and ask her. She's reasonable. Most days."

*B*renda didn't have an alarm clock in her bedroom. It was the smell of the coffee brewing that woke her. She'd brought herself one of those fancy coffee makers with a timer that magically poured her a cup each morning before the sun came up. Best purchase of her life.

She let the aroma lead her down the stairs like they were fingers in her nose, pulling her along. She was surprised her feet didn't come up off the ground as she made her way to the kitchen and the automatic coffee maker. Pulling two mugs from the cabinet, Brenda poured herself two cups. Like every day of her adult life, she would drink the first one down, letting the hot water burn her tongue and wake up all her brain cells. By the time she finished the first, the second one would be room temperature and ready to savor.

She reached in the fridge for the milk. Only to put the pitcher back. She'd grabbed for the milk that had come straight from the cow instead of the skim milk.

Finally, with her double dose of caffeine in her veins, Brenda ran a brush through her hair. She lost the battle with the tangles, so she gathered her tresses into a ponytail. She pulled a clean shirt over her head and jeans up her legs. Stepping into her boots, she was out the door before the first rays of the new day sun poked over the horizon.

She pulled the notepad from the back of her pocket. Flipping open the pad, she surveyed her list. Most of her chores were the same every day. There was always bale to stack, bale to move, feed to grind, manure to haul, bills to pay, and a fence to fix.

The only fence she was worried over today was the fencing that kept her new prize bull in. She knew the beast was raring to get his job done. But that would have to wait. She had to wean the calves from their mothers and set the newly independent beasts out in their own pasture.

The rooster stretched his feathers as Brenda walked past the coop. He was a slacker like the rest of her ranch hands. None of which were there yet.

Instead of growling about it, Brenda got down to work. She had half her chores checked off her list before the sun blinked a ray open at the horizon.

Brenda climbed on the tractor. It was an older model, older than her. But it worked just fine. She jammed in the specialized key, better known as a screwdriver. The actual key had been lost months ago, somewhere out in her vast acreage. The engine turned over immediately, and she got to work.

By the time she'd worked the land and brought the tractor back, her ranch hands had finally shown up. Late. Again.

Just because she was a woman, they thought they could take advantage of her. Also, because it was late in the season, and most ranch hands had already been hired. She'd gotten the scraps of workers. Manuel was a holdover from her grandfather's time. His nephew was a good worker when he was away from his uncle's gnarled guidance. The other two were pretty much useless outside of being able to lift heavy things. She'd done more this morning than all four of them combined had done all week.

Brenda put the tractor in park. She remembered the specialized key and put it to work at its third job of the day. Twisting her ponytail into a bun, she jammed the screwdriver into her tresses. To keep her hair out of her face. And off her shoulders. And, yes, potentially as a weapon for what she had to do.

"You're late," she said. "Again."

Manuel grinned. "Sorry, honey. But the cattle don't know the difference."

Brenda clenched her fists. But she didn't reach for the screwdriver. Yet. Though she was having very happy visions imagining Manuel's head as an ignition that needed help getting started. Actually, that wasn't far from the truth. The man was stuck in the dark ages of ranching. He needed a jumpstart. But Brenda was sure it was too late for him.

"I'm not your honey," she said calmly. "I'm your boss. But it doesn't look like I'll be that much longer."

"Don't tell me." Manuel's bushy brows lifted. His crooked grin rearranged his wrinkled face into something distasteful. "You're finally getting your-self a husband?"

The three younger men winced. No surprise there. All three of them were born into this genera-tion, where they'd seen women wield power and respect. Manuel was about to get a time and culture shock.

"Let me be clear," said Brenda. "Your services are no longer needed here on the ranch."

Manuel's face contorted into something ugly. It reminded Brenda of the bull receiving his brand. The hiss of pain. The shock of betrayal. The shudder of resignation.

Brenda braced for Manuel to lash out. But he held still. It was the three men behind him that fidgeted like nervous newborn foals.

"You firing me, missy?"

"Good." Brenda stretched her lips into a cruel grin to match his. "I don't have to use smaller words."

His shoulders snapped straight. His fists curled. His mustache twitched. Dark shadows moved across his face as he dipped his head low so that his hat shielded his gaze.

Brenda held her ground. This was her ranch. It was her livelihood on the line. They all could go and find other work, with a man whom they might respect.

Or not. She didn't care. All she cared about was the running of and respect for her ranch.

"Now see here, Miss Vance."

Yeah! He had finally used the word *miss* appropriately. If she had a gold star, she still wouldn't give it to him. Too little, too late. He'd failed. And he was getting expelled.

"Without us, you have no hope of keeping this ranch up and running. It's calving season. It's not a one-man job. Definitely not a job for a woman."

The multitude of checkmarks on the list in her back pocket would beg to differ. But he was right. She couldn't do it all on her own. She would need a hand. Just not his.

She might've trained the younger three. But with the gnarled hand of Manuel having brainwashed them, they were as useless to her as a castrated bull.

"It is no longer your concern," she said.

Manuel curled his lip. His mustached twitched, making him look like the villain in some cartoon. Part of Brenda wanted to laugh. Instead, she looked behind him to see if she might salvage anything.

"If any of you lot are interested in staying, I'm willing to consider retraining."

There was a spark in each of their eyes. Well, the two city boys' eyes. Angel looked away, hiding his feelings on the matter from his uncle and Brenda alike. But Brenda took that as answer enough.

"They won't be led by your apron strings," said

Manuel. "You won't make it a week without us. Let's go, boys. We get a weeklong break before she comes crawling back."

The two city boys looked at each other. Then they shuffled back to Manuel's truck. From the corner of her eye, Brenda caught Angel's wince. But he fell in line and trudged back to the truck as well.

"There are no hands available at this time in the season," Manuel said to her. "Can't wait to see you on your knees when you come begging for help."

"Why don't you hold your breath waiting for that to happen," she said.

With a youthful grace that belied his wrinkles, Manuel hopped into the driver's seat and took off. Brenda was about to let out a sigh of relief. She also let the floodgates of worry and anxiety about what she would do open. He was right. Help would be hard to find at this point in the season.

And then the truck stopped. Brenda used her hand to shield her eyes as she peered at the back of the truck. It was halfway to the gate to her property.

Had they come to their senses? Did they want to come back and play by her rules? Would she allow it?

Before she could answer any of those internal questions, Manuel hopped out. He lifted his booted foot and kicked at a weak spot in the fencing. It was the bullpen. The pen that housed her new, pricey bull.

Manuel tipped his hat, hopped back in, and peeled out of her ranch.

The bull was at the center of the pen, and his back was turned. Brenda knew that she wasn't going to make it in time before he escaped. But she had to try. Any damage he might cause, she would be liable for, and she couldn't afford it.

She moved quick. Grabbing a sack of grain with one hand and a bag of sugar with the other, she hopped back on the tractor. She pulled the key from her hair and jammed it into the ignition.

The tractor stalled. She tried again. The bull had turned and was walking gingerly toward the broken fence.

Finally, the engine turned over. Brenda took off. But at twenty miles per hour, she was already too late. Her only hope was to corral the bull before he could hurt himself or anyone else.

Off in the distance, she saw a Jeep turn into her gates. A red Jeep. A red Jeep headed straight toward her bull.

Who drove a red Jeep on a cattle ranch? Of

course, Brenda knew that bulls were color blind. But it was a superstition nonetheless.

Brenda gunned the tractor, topping twenty-five miles per hour. She was too late. The bull spotted the red Jeep and rammed into it.

CHAPTER FIVE

Keaton had taken many hits in his lifetime. He'd studied Brazilian Jiu Jitsu where he'd been lifted and thrown bodily across a five-point ring. He'd been kicked in the chest during hand to hand combat training. He'd even had a round hit him in his body armor.

Each hit had rattled him. Each impact had made his vision go blurry. Had made his thoughts scatter, but never too far. Each time, he'd quickly regained his equilibrium and was back in fighting form within a few seconds, a moment at the max.

The great beast barreling toward him was bigger than the pro wrestlers and martial artists he'd faced in the ring. Its hooves tore up the ground each time its feet kicked against the earth to push it faster toward Keaton. Both vehicle and bull were going at the same speed, though the bull may have had a couple of miles on Keaton's Jeep.

In any case, Keaton was not going to outrun this fate. He did the only thing he could. He braced for impact.

Which was a mistake. Tense muscles and tense bones were more prone to injury than relaxed ones. But there was no way he was about to relax. There was an eight-hundred-pound bull headed straight for his driver's side door.

The metal door was no comparison to the armor plate inside a bulletproof vest. Car manufacturers had yet to make a bull proof, well, anything. Metal crunched as the door bent to the bull's will.

Keaton felt the impact on his shoulder and right side. But it was the booming crash that rattled him. The sound ripped his sense of equilibrium in half. He felt that the rug that had been pulled out from under him was the rug on the floor of the entire world.

The bull clearly felt the effects, too. It stood outside the door of the Jeep. Stunned. Its eyes were unblinking. Its breathing slow and ragged. For all the damage it caused the jeep, Keaton was sure the bull had to be bleeding internally.

A dust trail in the distance caught his attention. A tractor was coming toward him. Behind the wheel sat what he could only describe as an Amazonian warrior.

Long, brown hair flew behind her. Her toned arms had the type of muscles a woman got from a hard day's work and not in choreographed kicks and twists at the gym. Her lips were pursed with concentration. Her gaze was focused. Keaton felt the urge to know what the color that determined gaze was.

Instinctively, his hand reached for the door to let him out of the Jeep. He pushed, but the door only went a couple of inches. Not enough for him to scoot his body out.

"Stay put," the warrior woman shouted.

There was so much command in her voice that Keaton did as he was told. The avenging angel put the tractor in park. She leaped out the door before the wheels came to a full stop. Her motion slowed, and it was as though he was watching one of those action movies with the slowed-down fast motion.

No. It wasn't her motion that was slow. It had to be his brain.

He knew she moved quickly, efficiently. But his eyes seemed to want to linger on her motions. Each action she took, his brain set up the replay, like in a football game when a play had to be reviewed.

Her hands raised slowly. Her voice was soothing, calming. Her words were pretty but unintelligible. But their meaning was clear.

Relax.

Everything's okay.

Come with me.

I'll make it better.

Keaton's whole being relaxed. All the pain from the impact dissipated. He was absolutely going to come with this woman who promised to make him better. He felt like a better man just being in her presence.

He tried to open the car door again. Again, it barely budged. Time returned to normal speed, and he caught a flash. It was his warrior angel. She'd flashed her eyes up at him.

They were green, by the way. Green like a blade of grass. A sharp blade of grass that just might leave a nasty cut. So, why did he have the urge to roll around in the pastures of her gaze?

"It's okay, big guy," she said.

Her voice had a dulcet quality. But it was soft as if the feathers were made of steel. It made Keaton's spidey senses tingle. Not over his skin like a premonition of danger. This sensation went straight into his bloodstream like it was a shot of adrenaline. Again, he tried to make his way out of the Jeep and to her.

"I've got this, soldier," she said.

"Let me help," he said.

"You're not part of the plan."

Keaton frowned at that. A plan that he was not a part of? It did not compute. He added a new item to his to-do list; get on board with this warrior angel's plan. Whatever it may be.

Her plan looked like she was going to corral the stunned bull back through the gaping hole in the fence. With a bag of grain and white granules that looked like salt, or maybe sugar.

The bull shook its head as though it was waking from a dream. It blinked a couple of times and then focused on her. Its nostrils puffed out gusts of air.

Was it going to ram her? It had already run into Keaton. He knew at that moment that he would die before he let anything hurt this woman. Whatever her original plan, Keaton was instituting Plan B.

He shoved out of the vehicle. Only for his back to hit the Jeep's door at her annoyed demand that he stay put. He ignored that. His boots hit the ground.

Followed by his knees.

And then his shoulders.

And, finally, his head.

The last thing Keaton realized before he passed out was that the white granules she'd tossed at the bull weren't salt. They were sugar. He wondered if he kissed her pouting, disapproving lips if she would taste as sweet?

"I was able to stop the internal bleeding." Maggie Banks gathered her tools and began placing them back in her veterinarian's bag. "He's going to take a while to heal, which means he's definitely going to be out of commission for the breeding season."

Brenda pressed both her thumbs to her temples. The other four fingers she raised to the Heavens as though in prayer. For guidance? For patience? For a miracle? Probably all three.

As if her short handedness wasn't enough. Now, her prized bull, which she'd sunk most of her liquid cash in, was useless. How was she going to make more babies to replace the cows she would have to separate from the herd and sell? And find the help to do it? Manuel was right. With the size of her herd, this was not a one-man job.

Letting out a moan, Brenda dropped her hands. Her voice was rough and deep. It appeared to have gotten deeper with the hole she was now in. No, that sound hadn't come from her. It had come from the soldier whose jeep had been the unlucky matador's cape in this debacle.

Brenda had propped him up in the shade against the fence. She was a strong woman, but he had been far too heavy to lug inside. He was a big guy, but definitely not out of shape. He had thick legs made for horseback riding, though he clearly hadn't been near a horse lately if a Jeep was his mode of transportation in cattle country and farmland. His arms were the type that could wrap around a barrel and lift it. But she bet he'd likely been using those guns to carry, well, guns. His shirt had come untucked when he'd collapsed, and Brenda had been treated to a view of his six-pack.

Suddenly, she was thirsty for a beer to cool down. From all the exertion. Of corralling the bull.

Her cheeks were obviously flushed because of her anger at her former ranch hands. Still, the cold beer sounded good. But that would have to wait until after her bull was tended to.

"Can I check on *him* now?" asked Maggie.

Maggie had tried to tend to the soldier first, him being a human and all. Brenda had waited impatiently, insisting the man was still breathing, and that was the best they could do. Now that her bull was stable, she gave a head nod, acquiescing that Maggie could turn her attention to the man.

"Sergeant Keaton?" said Maggie.

The man blinked, opening groggy eyes. Cloudy like the sky after a storm. That was Brenda's favorite time; after the rain had washed away all the dirt and dust and left behind a fresh slate. After a storm was the time when things could begin anew. A fresh start. Because the worst had been done.

Sergeant Keaton fixed his clear-eyed gaze on Brenda. There wasn't any hint of cloud. In his eyes, Brenda saw the perfect fresh start.

Brenda felt corralled by his look like her entire body would go wherever he directed. Which was nuts. It had to be that weird Purple Heart Ranch hoodoo. He and Maggie must have brought it onto her land. Well, they'd be getting up and getting off her land soon. She had no need of a husband.

"How many fingers am I holding up?" asked Maggie.

Sergeant Keaton blinked, turning his clear eyes

away from Brenda. His gaze went hazy as he looked at Maggie's two fingers. He canted his head, leaning away to peer around Maggie's hand at Brenda.

"Are you okay?" he asked.

Was she okay? He was the one that casually bumped into an eight-hundred-pound bull. And he was asking about her.

"It didn't get you, did it?" he asked.

"The bull?" said Brenda. "No. He got you. And your Jeep."

Brenda's thumbs went back to her temples. Her fingers straightened back up to Heaven. But she knew no miracle was forthcoming to take care of the damage her bull had done to that car. Legally, she was responsible. Even though it was Manuel's maliciousness. Unfortunately, that argument wouldn't hold up in court.

Her land. Her bull. Her responsibility.

"Look," she said, dropping her thumbs when the throbbing continued all around the crown of her head. "I'll file an insurance claim for your vehicle and cover your medical bills."

It would set her back even more. But it was the law. It was also the right thing to do. And her parents had raised her to do right.

"I'm fine," said Sergeant Keaton.

He shifted his big body, trying to get his feet under him. As he leaned forward, Brenda got a clear sight of a strong chest with a dusting of fine hair. Even though his pectorals looked like they were solid as a rock, she was willing to bet that they'd be soft as pillows if she were to rest her weary head upon them.

"Brenda," grunted Maggie, "a little help?"

"Hunh?" Brenda blinked. "Oh. Right."

Maggie had grabbed one side of the soldier. Brenda rushed to his other side. Instead of focusing on righting himself, he grinned down at Brenda.

"You're strong," he said.

"You're weak," she said.

"Am not." He frowned. "I can do fifty-eight pushups, sixty-nine sit-ups, and run five miles in a half-hour."

"Those are the requirements to pass the Army Ranger exam," said Maggie.

"It's not an exam," said Sergeant Keaton. "It's a test of physical fitness, which you can't pass if you're weak."

"Well," said Brenda. "I bet those are great in the army. But they mean nothing on a ranch."

"Can you complete a twelve-mile march with a thirty-five-pound pack on your back?"

"No, but I can drive a herd of cattle ten miles with nothing but a length of rope and a sidearm."

They stood toe to toe now. Sergeant Keaton had a head over Brenda. Brenda was tall. She wasn't used to guys being on her level. Definitely not above it. Despite her attempts to knock him down a peg, she had the feeling she'd met her match.

"Sergeant Keaton," said Maggie. "You should take it easy. You were just in an accident."

"I promise I'm fine." He didn't take his eyes off Brenda as he made the assertion. "No need to file any forms. The car is insured. I got the accident plan."

He did? The one that rental car companies tried to scare customers into purchasing before they handed over the keys even though it was unlikely they'd ever need it? Brenda got the feeling a man like Sergeant Keaton wouldn't fall for that. She had the suspicion that he'd bought the accident insurance on purpose.

Who does that?

"I feel fine," he continued. "But, I'll get checked out by the doctors at the Purple Heart Ranch if it'll stop you two from glaring at me."

Well, that was a load off of Brenda's checkbook. She'd take him up on it. Now, she had two fewer bills to pay. But that didn't answer the question that had been nagging her since she'd seen his Jeep in the distance.

"What are you doing here?" she asked. "Did you get lost?"

"No," he said, testing his balance by stretching those bulging arm muscles. "This is where I'm meant to be."

Something about that statement sent a tingle down her spine. It had the ring of truth to it.

"Meant to be what?" she asked.

"I was looking for you."

"Me?"

"I need something from you."

"From me?" Her voice sounded breathy to her own ears. Brenda was never breathy. And definitely not for some guy. But her breathing was shallow as she hung on his every word.

"I need your land," he said.

The air slapped into her lungs from the gasp. The quick inflation made her head light. All the warmth went cold.

"Just the edge of it," he went on. "Where the creek is. I'll pay its value if I can get it by the end of the week."

The creek? At value? That would be enough to

secure her debts, buy another bull, and maybe even hire a decent ranch hand or two.

"You got yourself a deal," said Brenda.

She stuck out her hand. Sergeant Keaton took it gingerly. When his fingers closed around hers, she felt a zing. The force was like the kick from a bull. By the look on his face, she knew he felt it too.

But they'd both been taken down by the same bull.

That was all it was.

CHAPTER SEVEN

"The deal is a no go."

Keaton sat in State Senator, Ginger Chase's office. The pretty blonde stared at her computer screen. Her fingers flew on the keyboard as though she were chasing after the insurgent that was standing in their way. But Keaton's attention was on the beautiful brunette next to him.

Brenda Vance had changed out of her jeans and T-shirt and into a nicer pair of jeans and a blouse. The new jeans were a darker blue and played perfectly against her tanned skin. The blouse, which was buttoned all the way up, still showcased the line of her neck, making Keaton's mouth thirst.

She'd driven them into town in her old Ford F150. The AC had worked, so she'd rolled the windows up and put the radio on. It had been for the best. Keaton was at a loss as to what to say to the woman. Brenda seemed perfectly content with the silence between them. So, he'd closed his eyes and let her take the wheel.

Keaton's rental car company had arrived and towed the ruined Jeep back into town. The owner hadn't been happy when he remembered that Keaton had taken out the insurance policy. Of course, he'd taken out the insurance policy. What responsible adult wouldn't?

Since the rental car company was on the same street alongside the city council building, he and Brenda had decided to kill two birds with one stone and stopped in. No appointment was necessary, as Maggie Banks had called ahead. Ginger was family, she'd said. However, Keaton didn't see any physical resemblance.

"I swear with the backward ordinances in this town, it's a wonder anyone stays here." Ginger's husband, Sergeant Colin Chase, leaned over his wife's chair.

Ginger turned her face up to his. "It kept you here."

"You kept me here," Chase countered.

Keaton looked away as the newlyweds made

otter eyes at each other. Chase had come with his team to the Purple Heart Ranch nearly a year ago to find healing and rehabilitation after a mission gone wrong. Now, each of the four-man Fire Team was living on or near the ranch in wedded bliss.

The happiness and love between the two were palpable. It was nice; having someone who you could both depend on, and then go on and kiss. A soft place to fall at the end of a hard mission. Keaton wondered if maybe he'd move his five-year plan up a year or two. Maybe he could make time for dating even sooner.

His gaze latched onto Brenda as she leaned forward in the seat beside him. Her lips twisted in impatience as she cleared her throat. It took a second, and a louder throat clearing, for the lip-locked married couple to focus on the matter at hand.

"You're saying I can't sell my land to a willing buyer because of some ordinance?" asked Brenda.

"No, you can," said Ginger. "Just not as quickly as you'd like. The sale will take six months to go through. And in that time, no new construction can take place by anyone but the owner."

That caught Keaton's attention and broke his study of Brenda Vance's lips. "I need to be up and running in ninety days. My guys will be here tomorrow. We need to break ground by the end of the week to stay on schedule."

He'd planned for some setbacks. But not any of this magnitude. Six months? They couldn't afford to wait around for six months. They'd lose all their contracts, the contracts that would set the business into the black. He hadn't gone to the government to gain land for this very reason. The bureaucratic red tape took time to unravel. But here it was rearing its sticky head.

"There has to be a way around this," said Keaton, his brain already going into tactical overdrive, trying to suss out a workaround.

"Well," said Chase. "There is one way that I can think of."

Both Brenda and Keaton leaned forward eagerly. Before Chase responded, he glanced at his wife. The two shared a knowing look. It was the same silent communication Keaton had with Grizz when they were about to slip into some hairy business on the battlefield. Except there was adoration in this couple's look. Not an any-last-words kinda look he'd often exchanged with his best friend.

Keaton had never had a connection like that with a woman. One where words weren't needed. He'd learned communication was key with the fairer sex. But at the same time, women didn't like blunt honesty.

Whatever nonverbal words transpired between Ginger and Chase, they clearly understood each other perfectly and were on the same page.

Another glance at Brenda and Keaton got the impression she'd clued in on this silent exchange. Her expression changed from eager interest to total denial. She was also no longer leaning forward. She had pressed her body back into the chair, as though she was trying to get as far away as possible from the couple and their impending words.

What was going on?

"If you two are thinking what I think you're thinking …" Brenda waved her finger at them. Then she waved both hands, as though warding them off. Then she huffed and crossed her arms over her chest in the universal language of back off. "Then, don't even."

Ginger and Chase only smiled. From the little he knew of Brenda Vance, Keaton knew she wasn't a woman who rattled easily. She'd faced down a bull with only a bag of grain and sugar. But looking at her in the chair, she looked completely rattled.

"What's going on?" Keaton asked the question to

Brenda. He wondered if he'd get the message looking into her eyes. But she wouldn't meet his gaze.

"There has to be another way," said Brenda.

"We could get the law changed," said Ginger. "But that would take even longer."

"What if I leased the land to him instead of selling it?" asked Brenda.

"That could work, but it would still take time. Less time. Maybe two to three months before any construction could start."

"Neither of those options work for me," said Keaton. "We have a client booked for ninety days from now. They'll put us in the black for the whole year. We have to be ready, or we'll lose the contract."

He looked around the room. Ginger looked sympathetic. Chase looked amused. Brenda looked furious.

"What's this other way you're not telling me about?" Keaton said.

Keaton directed his comment to Chase. Chase looked to his wife. Ginger looked at Brenda. Brenda threw up her hands and faced Keaton.

"They're suggesting we get married," said Brenda.

Indignation rang through her voice. Her fingers

flicked at the air like she was brushing the ridiculous notion aside. The corners of her eyes crinkled, and her brow creased as though the idea was insane.

But Keaton's brain was working, adjusting his master plan. Suddenly, the notion of waiting five years to find the perfect woman didn't seem so necessary. It wasn't ridiculous that he could squeeze Brenda into the plan. He could shift some things around.

Which was insane. Right? It had to be the bump on his head from the bull. Right? Even though the idea made his head stop hurting and his heart race.

CHAPTER EIGHT

"This town is absolutely insane." Brenda glared at the flashing red Don't Walk light. She tapped her foot impatiently as the light counted down. Counting was not going to calm her down. She needed to find a green light to get this moving.

"Yeah," Keaton sighed.

He stood beside her on the street corner. He'd had nothing but monosyllabic answers since they'd stormed out of Ginger's office. Well, she had stormed. He'd followed her, walking quietly in his combat boots. Too bad. Brenda was sure they'd sound like thunder rolling in if he was stomping mad.

Why wasn't he stomping mad?

His plans were being thwarted by bureaucratic red tape that should not hold up in a court of law. He clearly wasn't from this part of the country. Even though his muscles looked like they were crafted for bull wrangling.

But the way he carried himself, the straightness of his spine told her he spent more time in taxicabs and Ubers than crouched over a fast running horse. The way his grin held just a little back, as though he hadn't known his neighbors all his life, or maybe he hadn't met each of the people that lived around him. That told her that there stood a city boy through and through.

The light changed to green. Before she stepped into the street, Keaton crossed behind her. His fingers ghosted her low back. Not touching. But close enough that she could feel their impression. Once he was on the side of the street closest to the waiting cars, he fell back into step with her.

He had country manners. A man should always place his body between traffic and a woman. It was a ridiculous notion because if a car jumped the curb, it was barreling into both of them. But the thought was nice.

"Sometimes, I hate this town," said Brenda. "At every turn, someone is insisting you get married. Be it in church, on the Purple Heart Ranch, or at the kitchen table."

If it wasn't her former ranch hand, then it was her brother. If it wasn't her brother, then it was the city government.

"I see," said Keaton.

Two words this time. So, progress.

Keaton shoved his hands in his pockets and hunched his shoulders. He hadn't looked at her since leaving Ginger Chase's office. They still didn't have a viable solution to this mess.

Clearly, marriage was out of the question. It wasn't even a question. The people in this town needed to stop trying to solve business issues with matrimony. It wasn't that easy.

"What if it was that easy?" said Keaton, coming to a stop.

"What if what were that easy?" Brenda asked as she turned to face him.

Keaton's gaze was fixed upon the building in front of them. They were standing at the City Hall. The building was a two-story affair. The mayor and his staff occupied the top floor. On the ground floor was where most civic matters were taken care of. Things like filing lawsuits, paying for violations, and getting marriage licenses.

Brenda's gaze jerked from the building and back to the man standing toe to toe with her.

"What if we did it?" he said.

"Did what?" She couldn't voice it. She could barely even think it. But her mind was already getting away from her.

"What if we got married?"

"Maybe we should stop by the ER," said Brenda. "That was a pretty bad hit you took."

Keaton only grinned. It was a full grin, the kind she was sure he'd give to someone he'd known a lifetime. Why was he giving it to her when he hadn't known her for a day?

It was a dangerous grin. A grin she wouldn't mind seeing for a lifetime. Every self-preserving bone in Brenda's body told her to take a step back from him. Brenda held perfectly still under the assault of that heart-stopping grin.

"I'm fine," Keaton said. "I'm thinking clearly. I'm thinking logically."

He ran a hand through his hair. It wasn't exactly a buzz cut. Which meant he'd been out of the service long enough to let it grow. Brenda wondered what his hair would look like if the locks touched his ears. She wondered what it would feel like if her fingertips brushed the wayward strand of hair that fell onto his forehead.

"Is there really much difference between a marriage contract and a leasing agreement?" he asked. "In a sense, it's all about ownership."

"But in marriage, you would own my property and me."

Something flashed in his gaze. Like a predator flashing his pupils in the dark at helpless prey. Brenda wasn't easy prey. She was always armed. Not with a screwdriver at the moment. But she had her wits about her.

"I would never take anything from you," he said. "I want to build something."

That statement nearly disarmed her. He was a wily one. She'd need to keep her eyes on him. Oh, this man was dangerous. Did she need the money enough to get tangled up with the likes of him?

"We're two grown adults," he said. "Both business savvy from what I can see of your ranch. You were methodical in how you dealt with that loose bull. At least, what I remember of the incident."

His grin went cocky this time. His teeth flashed white at her. Her self-preservation instincts were going haywire. Part of her wanted to run. The confusion was in figuring out the direction. Because most of her body was urging her to crash right into that strong chest and test it for pliability.

"I'm a planner, too," he continued. "Maybe we'd work well together."

Had sexier words ever been uttered by any other man in existence? A man with a plan. And he wanted to partner up. She wondered if he used an old fashioned checklist? Or was he not into paper planners and used a digital organizer on his phone?

Brenda gave herself a shake. Was she seriously talking about marriage? With a stranger? This was not a viable path.

"How can you think we work well together?" she said. "The only evidence we have is from when I told you to stay in the Jeep. You bucked my plan and got out anyway."

Keaton winced. "I didn't understand your plan then. I've told you mine. Tell me yours. Why did you agree to the sale so quickly?"

Brenda swallowed, but the words still escaped her throat. "I need help."

That's not what she'd meant to say. But it came out nonetheless

"I mean the money will help," she tried to course correct. "I've mechanized a lot of the ranch operations. But I still need ranch hands to work with the cattle. And now I'm going to need a new bull for breeding."

"I can help with that," he said. "The hands, I mean. There are six of us. Highly trained Army Rangers. We've been put in tough situations before and came out alive."

"Any of those tough situations happen on a ranch?"

"No, but we're adaptable. Think about it. If we get married, all we'd need is a prenup stating you're entitled to the money for the sale of the creek, and I'm entitled to keep the creek. No other paperwork would be necessary. It's a good plan, and we could both put it into action by the end of the week."

He made it all sound so simple. Brenda would get the money she needed immediately. Plus, free labor. Where was the downside?

These nuptials are about to be anything but convenient. Watch how Brenda and Keaton get married and then fall inconveniently in love in
The Rancher takes his Convenient Bride,
Book One in the Rangers of Purple Heart Ranch.

Shanae Johnson was raised by Saturday Morning cartoons and After School Specials. She still doesn't understand why there isn't a life lesson that ties the issues of the day together just before bedtime. While she's still waiting for the meaning of it all, she writes stories to try and figure it all out. Her books are wholesome and sweet, but her are heroes are hot and heroines are full of sass!

And by the way, the E elongates the A. So it's pronounced Shan-aaaaaaaa. Perfect for a hero to call out across the moors, or up to a balcony, or to blare outside her window on a boombox. If you hear him calling her name, please send him her way!

You can sign up for Shanae's Reader Group at http://bit.ly/ShanaeJohnsonReaders

Also By Shanae Johnson

The Brides of Purple Heart

On His Bended Knee

Hand Over His Heart

Offering His Arm

His Permanent Scar

Having His Back

In Over His Head

Always On His Mind

Every Step He Takes

In His Good Hands

Light Up His Life

Strength to Stand

The Rangers of Purple Heart

The Rancher takes his Convenient Bride

The Rancher takes his Best Friend's Sister

The Rancher takes his Runaway Bride

The Rancher takes his Star Crossed Love

The Rancher takes his Love at First Sight

The Rancher takes his Last Chance at Love

The Silver Star Ranch Romances

His Pledge to Honor

His Pledge to Cherish

His Pledge to Protect

His Pledge to Have

His Pledge to Hold

www.ingramcontent.com/pod-product-compliance
Lightning Source LLC
Chambersburg PA
CBHW061247120726

48001CB00001B/184